Lexile: 669

I should have run when Lucas stepped over to me, but I didn't. I stood there gazing into his silver eyes. They held me captive. They wouldn't let me look away. I felt this strange pull. I wanted to lean into him. I wanted to wrap myself around him. Around Lucas, who always made me feel like I wanted to crawl out of my skin.

He wrapped his hands around my arms. I thought he would jerk me toward him now and plant that kiss that I so desperately wanted.

Instead he said solemnly, "Kayla, you're one of us."

OTHER BOOKS BY
RACHEL HAWTHORNE

The Boyfriend League
Caribbean Cruising
Island Girls (and Boys)
Labor of Love
Love on the Lifts
Snowed In
Suite Dreams
Thrill Ride

RACHEL HAWTHORNE

MOONLIGHT

A DARK GUARDIAN NOVEL

HARPERTEEN

AN IMPRINT OF HARPERCOLLINS*PUBLISHERS*

HarperTeen is an imprint of HarperCollins Publishers.

Dark Guardian: Moonlight
Text copyright © 2009 Jan Nowasky
www.harperteen.com

Library of Congress Cataloging in Publication Data
Hawthorne, Rachel.
    Moonlight / Rachel Hawthorne. — 1st ed.
        p.   cm. — (Dark Guardian)
    Summary: While working as a wilderness guide in the national forest where her parents were killed twelve years earlier, seventeen-year-old Kayla is powerfully drawn to Lucas, who she learns is her appointed guardian—and much more—as she discovers her true identity and destiny.
    ISBN 978-0-06-170955-5
    [1. Supernatural—Fiction.   2. Werewolves—Fiction.
3. Identity—Fiction.   4. Wilderness areas—Fiction.   5. Forest guides (Persons)—Fiction.   6. Orphans—Fiction.]   I. Title.
PZ7.H31374Moo   2009   2008045066
[Fic]—dc22   CIP
                                                          AC

Typography by Andrea Vandergrift
10 11 12 13   LP/RRDH   10 9 8 7 6 5
❖
First Edition

For Alex, werewolf and tattoo advisor extraordinaire.
Thanks for all the brainstorming lunch sessions and for
answering my questions at two in the morning.
You rock! Love, Mom

Moonlight washed over us, washed over Lucas and me.

A hushed silence permeated the forest. Giant trees surrounded us. Their rustling leaves whispered warnings in the warm breeze of the summer night. But we ignored them. We cared only about one another.

He was much taller than I was, and I had to bend my head back to gaze into his silver eyes. They were hypnotic, which should have calmed my racing heart but instead only made it speed up. Or maybe it was the nearness of his lips that sent my heart into a chaotic rhythm.

He took a step closer and I retreated, but a tree stopped me from going as far away as I wanted. Was I ready for this? Was I ready for a kiss that would change my life? I knew that if he kissed me I'd never be the same again. That *we* would never be the same. That our relationship would shift—

My mind stuttered with the enormity of such a simple word. *Shift*. It meant more to me now—now that I understood.

Lucas was suddenly nearer. I hadn't seen the movement. He was just there. He could move that quickly. My knees grew weak, and I was grateful that I had a sturdy tree to lean against. He lifted his arm and pressed his forearm against the bark over my head as though he, too, needed some sort of support. The action brought him even closer. I felt the welcoming heat of his body reaching out to mine. Under normal circumstances he would have drawn me in for a comforting snuggle, but nothing about tonight was normal.

He was beautiful in the moonlight. Gorgeous, really. His thick, straight hair—a medley of colors: white, black, and silver, with a little brown thrown in for good measure—hung down to his shoulders. I had this reckless urge to touch it, to touch him.

But I knew any movement on my part would be a signal to him, a signal that I was ready. And I wasn't. I didn't want what he was offering. Not tonight. Maybe not ever.

What was I afraid of? It was only a kiss. I'd kissed other guys. I'd kissed Lucas.

So why did the thought of a kiss from Lucas tonight terrify me? The answer was simple: I knew this kiss would bind us together forever.

His fingers gently brushed my hair back from my brow. He'd once told me the shade of it reminded him of a fox. He thought of everything in terms related to the forest. It suited him and his solitary ways.

Why was he so patient? Why didn't he push? Did he feel it, too? Did he understand how momentous it would be if—

He dipped his head down. I didn't move. I barely breathed. In spite of all my reservations, I desired this. I craved it. But still I fought against it.

His lips were almost touching mine. Almost.

"Kayla," he murmured invitingly, and his warm breath caressed my cheek. "It's time."

Tears stung my eyes. I shook my head, refusing to acknowledge the truth of his words. "I'm not ready."

I heard an ominous, throaty growl in the distance. He stiffened. I knew he'd heard it, too. He shoved away from me and glanced over his shoulder. That's when I saw them: a dozen wolves restlessly prowling the perimeter of the clearing.

Lucas looked back at me, disappointment reflected in his silver eyes. "Then pick another. But you can't go through it alone."

He turned his back on me and began striding with

purpose toward the wolves.

"Wait!" I screamed after him.

But it was too late.

He started discarding his clothes with each quickening step. Then he was running. He leaped into the air—

By the time he hit the ground, he was a wolf. He'd transformed in the shimmering wink of time from boy to beast. He was as beautiful in wolf form as in human form.

He threw back his head and howled at the moon, the harbinger of change, the bringer of destiny. The anguished sound reverberated through me, called to me. I wrestled against answering, but the wildness that resided deep inside me was too strong, too determined to have its way.

I started running toward him. . . .

It was difficult to believe that less than two weeks ago, I was laughing and mocking the idea of werewolves actually existing.

And now I, Kayla Madison, was about to become one.

ONE

Less than two weeks earlier . . .

Fear. It was a living, breathing thing that resided inside me. Sometimes I could feel it prowling around, striving to break free. It journeyed with me now as Lindsey and I stalked through the national forest's dense thicket near midnight. But I'd become pretty good at hiding the panic. I didn't want Lindsey to think she'd made a mistake when she'd convinced me to work as a wilderness guide with her during the summer. I figured I could learn a few tricks from her about battling my inner demons. She took the meaning of adventuresome to a whole new level.

But still, coming alone to a place where wild things looked for tasty snacks was insane. It was even crazier that we hadn't told anyone. We'd kept quiet because leaving the barracks once the lights were out was reason for dismissal. After surviving a week of intensive training, I definitely didn't want to get fired the night before my first assignment.

I tightened my fingers around my weapon—a Maglite. My adoptive dad is a cop who taught me, like, a hundred ways to kill a man using a flashlight. Okay, so I'm prone to exaggeration, but still, he'd shown me a few self-defense moves.

Off to the side where the trees and brush were thickest, I heard a rustling noise.

"Shh! Wait up. What was that?" I whispered harshly.

Lindsey scanned her flashlight between the trees and into the darkness of the canopy of leaves above. While there was a crescent moon tonight, its light couldn't penetrate the thickness of the trees here. "What was *what*?"

My flashlight beam hit her as I swung it around. She flinched and held up a hand to protect her eyes from the harsh light. Her silky, white-blond hair reflected the light and appeared magical. She reminded me of a whimsical fairy, but I knew her delicate features hid an inner strength. She'd been featured in the local paper because she'd saved a child from a cougar attack by putting herself between the animal and the child and yelling at it until it ran off.

"I thought I heard something," I told her.

"Like what?"

"I don't know." My heart thudding, I glanced around again. I loved the outdoors. But tonight, being out here gave me the creeps. I couldn't shake the feeling that I was being watched or having a *Blair Witch Project* moment.

"Like footsteps?" Lindsey asked.

"Not really. Not like a person makes. More a soft plodding, like walking in your socks—or on paws maybe."

Lindsey slung her arm easily around my slender shoulders. She was a little taller than I was, and her muscles were firm from all the hiking and rock climbing she did. We'd met last summer when I'd come camping with my parents. Lindsey had been one of our guides—or sherpas, as the park personnel referred to them. We'd connected and become fast friends, keeping in touch over the school year.

"We're not being followed," Lindsey assured me. "Everyone was asleep when we left our cabin."

"What if it's some kind of predator?" This fear I was experiencing didn't make sense. But I knew I'd heard something, and I knew it wasn't friendly. I couldn't explain how I knew—just a sixth sense sort of thing.

Lindsey's laughter echoed through the trees.

"I'm serious. What about that cougar you chased off last summer?" I asked.

"What about him?"

"What if he's out for revenge?"

"Then he'll eat me, not you. Unless he's just hungry. Then he'll eat whoever runs the slowest."

Which would be me, I thought. I wasn't exactly athletically challenged, but I wasn't *American Gladiators* material either.

I took a deep breath and listened intently. The woods were eerily quiet. Didn't they go silent when danger was near? "Maybe we should head back."

We were about a mile from the village that was at the entrance to the park. Lindsey and I shared a small cabin with Brittany, another guide. Once lights were out at eleven, no one was supposed to leave the cabin.

Now Lindsey imitated the sound of a chicken. *"Bawk! Bawk!"*

"Very funny. What if we get fired?" I asked.

"We'll only get fired if we get caught. Come on."

"What exactly is it that you want to show me?" All she'd told me was that she wanted to share "something intense" with me. It had been enough to make me curious, but that was when we were in the safety of the village.

"Look, Kayla, if you're going to be a sherpa, you have to connect with your inner adventure girl. Trust me. What I'm about to show you is well worth the risk of losing job, life, or limb."

"Wow. Really?" Was she dodging my question? It sure

seemed like it. I glanced around suspiciously. "Is the male of the species involved?" Because honestly, that's the only thing I considered worth the danger.

Lindsey sighed impatiently. "You're hopeless. Let's go."

Since I didn't want to be left alone, I fell into step beside her. As far as I was concerned, my caution was well earned. When I was five, my mom and dad were killed in these very woods. My adoptive parents had brought me here last summer to help me get over the trauma, which was probably a few years too late to really do any good. We'd camped here for nearly a week. I'd had an amazing time, but I wasn't sure how effective the experience had been in helping me to get over my "issues."

Yeah, supposedly I had emotional problems. So I was in therapy, spending a wasted hour each week with a shrink named Dr. Brandon, whose Yoda-like pronouncements—*face your fears, you must*—irritated more than helped me. Truly, I would have rather spent time with a dentist.

Maybe I was only kidding myself to think that I was brave enough to face the elements of the wild, day after day. Although what was I really afraid of? It wasn't even an animal that had attacked my parents. They'd been shot by two beer-guzzling hunters—in the woods illegally— who had stupidly mistaken them for wolves.

Thanks to those hunters, snarling, growling wolves regularly inhabited my dreams, resulting in many restless nights and frequent bouts of screaming in my sleep. Hence the therapy to get at the root of my nightmares. Dr. Brandon theorized that it was my subconscious trying to justify how two idiots could have shot my parents and then, with straight faces, tell authorities, "They were wolves. Swear to God, they were. They were gonna eat that little girl."

That little girl, of course, had been me. Everything that had happened on that long-ago afternoon was a blur. Everything except my parents lying dead on the forest floor.

God, how could they mistake people for wolves?

Behind me, brush crackled. I paused midstep. The hairs on my nape prickled. I slid my hand beneath the curtain of my red hair and rubbed my neck. A shiver went through me and goose bumps erupted over my arms. I had a feeling that if I turned around, I'd see whatever it was. Did I want to face it?

Lindsey tromped back. "What's wrong now?"

"Something's watching," I whispered. "I can feel it."

Lindsey didn't blow me off this time. She glanced around. "Could be an owl checking out a tasty morsel—or that late-night snack scampering away."

"Maybe, but it feels more sinister."

"Growing up down the road, I've spent most of my life in these woods. There's nothing sinister out here."

"What about the cougar?"

"That was way deep in the wilderness. We're still practically in civilization here. In a few areas you can still get cell phone reception." She tugged my hand. "A hundred steps and we'll be there."

I followed, but stayed alert. There was *something*. I was certain of it. Not an owl or a rodent. Not anything *in* the trees, not anything tiny. Something that stalked its prey.

A shudder rippled through me. *Prey?* Why had I thought that? But it was true. It was what I felt. Something was watching and waiting. But watching *whom* exactly? And waiting for *what*?

How many steps were left? Forty? It had been so stupid to come out without even telling anyone. My parents were going to kill me if they ever found out. I'd promised to be responsible. It was my first time away from them, and my adoptive mom had lectured me ad nauseam about being careful.

Up ahead, a brightness through the foliage caught my attention. "What's that?"

"What I wanted to show you."

We stepped between the trees and into a clearing, illuminated by a campfire. Before I could ask another question, a dozen kids—the other sherpas—leaped out from behind trees. "Surprise!" they yelled. "Happy birthday!"

My heart nearly stopped. I pressed a hand to my chest and laughed, grateful that it didn't sound hysterical. "My birthday isn't today."

"It's tomorrow, right?" Connor asked. He combed his sandy-blond hair off his brow to reveal his dark-blue eyes. He held up a wrist that sported a watch with numerous dials. "In ten seconds, nine, eight—"

The others joined in the countdown. I could see them clearly, standing in front of the fire. A short distance away from Connor was Rafe, with straight black hair that reached his shoulders and eyes a dark brown that bordered on black. He never said much. I was surprised he was actually counting.

"Seven, six—"

Beside him, Brittany looked almost like his twin. Her hair, falling past her shoulders, was black and her eyes were deep blue. She'd been asleep when we left. Or faking it, I realized. Yeah, trying to pull one over on me. She'd succeeded. *How did she get here ahead of us?* I wondered.

There were other sherpas, ones I'd met but not really connected with. Still, it meant a lot to me that they'd shown up to make tonight special.

"Five, four—"

At school, I'd always felt like an outsider. The girl who'd lost her parents. The adopted one. The one who didn't really belong. Jack and Terri Asher had taken me in. They weren't wicked stepparents or anything, but they just didn't always get me. But then, did any parents totally understand their kids?

"Three, two, one. Happy birthday!"

Connor moved around to the other side of the fire and crouched. A flame flared. Then a bottle rocket shot into the sky and exploded into a burst of red, white, blue, and green.

I was pretty sure that fireworks in a national forest were illegal. But I was too happy to care. Besides, I was free from parental restraints this summer. I wanted to finally test misbehavior boundaries.

"I can't believe you remembered!" I was so touched. Not even my few friends back home had ever thrown me a surprise party. I'd never minded because my natural parents had died on my birthday, so I always had mixed feelings about the day.

"Birthdays are important," Lindsey said. "Especially this one. Sweet seventeen."

Brittany extended a tray that held seventeen store-bought cupcakes, a candle in each one casting its yellow glow.

"I love cupcakes," I said, "especially the prepackaged, made-by-the-millions kind with the cream-filled center."

"Make a wish and blow them out."

I took a deep breath and leaned forward, and that's when I saw him.

Lucas Wilde.

He was leaning against a tree with his arms crossed over his broad chest, almost lost in the shadows as though he didn't want to be seen. But he had such a powerful presence that I was surprised he'd escaped my notice as long as he had. His eyes glowed silver in the darkness. As always, he was watching me intently.

Lucas terrified me. Okay, that wasn't exactly true. What I *felt for him* terrified me. It was an attraction that I couldn't quite explain. I'd had crushes on guys before, but what I felt with him went way beyond a crush. It was so strong that it was almost overwhelming—and a little bit embarrassing since obviously he wasn't returning the feelings. If anything, he tended to avoid direct contact with me. I tried to keep my feelings buried, but whenever I looked at him they would bubble to the surface and I was certain that he would see in my eyes what I fought so valiantly to control.

His nearness made my heart gallop and my mouth go dry. I wanted to comb my fingers through the long multicolored strands of his hair. When I'd first met him, I'd thought the unusual shade came from a bottle. I'd never seen anything like it. But then, I'd never seen anyone like him either. He was so intense. He'd been one of our tour guides last summer, but he'd seldom spoken to me. Still,

I often caught him watching me. It was as though he was waiting—

"Blow out the candles, already," Connor said.

His words snapped me back to the moment. I made my wish without thinking and then blew out the writhing flames with one big breath.

"Here you go," Brittany said, handing me a cupcake. "Sorry it isn't an official cake, but these are easier to serve in the wilderness."

"It's great," I said, beaming again, grateful for the distraction. "I wasn't expecting anything at all."

"We love surprises," Lindsey said. "But you guys could have been quieter getting here. She heard you. It almost ruined everything."

I playfully slapped Lindsey's arm. "That's what I heard?" Relief enveloped me, but at the same time, it didn't seem like the right explanation.

"Well, yeah, they had to be in bed when you and I left, so you wouldn't suspect anything, but they were supposed to hurry ahead to get things set up. And be quiet while doing it."

"But I heard something behind us, just before we got here."

"Like what?" Lucas asked, stepping away from the tree.

His deep voice sent a shiver of pleasure through me. It was just a voice and yet it touched me on a level I'd never experienced with anyone else. My absurd feelings made me self-conscious. I wasn't the type to attract guys who were as darkly handsome as Lucas was. Having his attention focused on me was unnerving, and suddenly I felt silly about my concerns. "I'm sure it was nothing."

"Then why mention it?"

"I didn't. Lindsey did."

I knew any normal girl would crave his attention. So why did he make me nervous? Why did my conversational skills take a hike when he was around?

"Relax, Lucas," Connor said. "It probably *was* us. You know how it is. When you try to be quiet, you end up making more noise."

But Lucas was staring at where we'd come from. If I didn't know better, I'd have thought he was sniffing the air. His nostrils flared and his chest expanded with the deep breath he took. "Maybe I should take a look around, just to be sure."

I knew he was nineteen, but he seemed older, maybe because he was a senior sherpa. He was the one in charge of our little group. If someone had a problem, he or she could go to Lucas. Although I'd probably let a wild bear eat me before I'd ask Lucas for help. Whether right or wrong, I suspected that he only respected those who solved their own problems. I had this absurd need to prove myself to him.

"Now you're as paranoid as Kayla," Lindsey said. "Grab a cupcake and sit down."

But Lucas didn't move. He kept his gaze on the path we'd taken to get here. It was strange but I knew if something had been following us, whatever it had been, Lucas would protect us from it. He just gave off those vibes. It was probably the reason that, as young as he was, he was given such authority and responsibility. He was so bold standing there that I didn't want to look away. But I also didn't want to give the impression that I was a lovesick kid.

Logs had been placed around the fire. I sat on one and peered over at Lucas. He was tall and in great shape. He wore his T-shirt like a second skin that outlined his muscles. I had this overwhelming urge to run my hands up those granite arms and across his shoulders. Pathetic. I was pathetic. He'd never given me any reason to think that he might return my interest.

"So what did your parents give you for your birthday?" Brittany asked, bringing my attention back to the others.

It didn't look as though anyone had noticed where my attention had wandered. Least of all Lucas. He always seemed so alert, I was surprised he wasn't aware of my assessment of him. On the other hand, it was also a relief that he gave me so little direct attention. Nothing was quite as embarrassing as one-sided obsession.

"A summer away from them." I grinned.

"They didn't seem *that* bad when I met them last year," Lindsey said.

"They're not," I admitted, taking the candle out of my cupcake and tossing it into the fire. "They're really pretty cool."

But they're not my real *parents.* I chided myself as soon as I thought those words. They were my real parents; they just weren't my original parents, from birth. Maybe what I'd sensed on our way here was the ghosts of my birth parents calling out to me. How silly was that explanation? I never had, never would believe in anything paranormal or supernatural.

"So what *did* they get you?" Brittany persisted.

"All the equipment I needed for a summer of trekking through the wilderness."

"No car?" Brittany asked.

"No car."

"Bummer."

"What difference does it make?" Connor asked. "Cars aren't allowed in the park."

Brittany gave him a sideways glance, then shrugged. "I guess."

There was something in her expression that I couldn't read, but it made me wonder if she liked Connor.

"Anyone else think this group we're taking out tomorrow is a little odd?" Rafe asked.

For a few minutes that afternoon, we'd all met Dr. Keane, his son, and several of the professor's grad students. We were going to escort them to a predetermined spot in the forest. Then we'd leave them for a couple of weeks before returning to retrieve them. They'd mentioned that they were hoping to spot some wolves.

"Odd in what way?" I asked.

"Dr. Keane is an anthropologist," Rafe said. "Why does he want to study wolves?"

"Wolves are certainly more interesting than people," Lindsey said. "Remember those wolf cubs we found when you were home for spring break, Lucas?"

"Yeah."

He was obviously a guy of few words, which only made him more intriguing—and intimidating at the same time. It was difficult to figure out what he thought about things, what he thought about me.

"They were the cutest," Lindsey went on, unperturbed by Lucas's lack of enthusiasm for the subject. "Orphaned. Three of them. We sort of adopted them until they were ready to go out on their own."

The other sherpas had all been working in the park at least a year. I should have felt like an outsider, but something about the group made me feel as though I belonged.

They weren't like the cliques at school. I'd never been part of those. I wasn't the wildly popular, cheerleader type. I wasn't a total math nerd, either. I wasn't quite sure I could actually define myself. Maybe that was the reason I was so comfortable out here. Everyone was the same: nature lovers appreciating the great outdoors.

Lucas shoved away from the tree. "We'd better head back."

"You're such a party pooper," Lindsey said.

"You'll thank me in the morning when you have to be ready to leave at dawn."

Everyone groaned with the reminder that we had an early morning. The guys put out the fire and flashlights came on.

I thanked everyone. "This was a great birthday surprise."

"Well, it's not every day you turn seventeen," Lindsey said. "We just wanted to do something special before we became preoccupied with surviving."

I laughed at her teasing. "It won't be that bad."

"The Keane party wants to go far into the woods, to an area we've never been before. The terrain will be rougher and we'll be pushed to the limits. Should be challenging," Brittany said.

Should be, I thought.

"Don't worry," Lindsey said to me. "You'll do great."

"I plan to give it my best."

We headed back up the trail to the rustic village where all the campers began their journey. Rafe was leading the way, with all the other sherpas scattered between him and me—except one. Lucas was following at the back of our group, right behind me. I had that sense of being watched again. A shudder rippled through me.

"What's wrong?" Lucas asked.

How had he known anything was wrong?

I glanced over my shoulder, feeling silly for saying it aloud. "Just that strange feeling that we're not alone."

"Yeah, I'm sensing it, too," he said, his voice low.

"Could it be those wolves you rescued?"

"I doubt it. The entrance to the park is too near civilization. Most of the wildlife is farther in."

That was in sync with what Lindsey had said about the cougar, but still—animals weren't always predictable.

Everyone in our group grew quiet, listening intently as we trudged along. The flashlights served as eerie beacons in the darkness. I was acutely aware of Lucas following closely behind me. Not that I could hear him—his footsteps were silent. But I sensed his nearness as though he were touching me—even though he wasn't. I felt nervous and excited. I wondered if he thought of me as anything other than the newbie. He'd never given any indication that he actually *liked* me in a romantic kind of way. Or

21

that he was interested in knowing me better. Here we had an opportunity to talk, and yet we both remained silent.

At the far end of the trail, more light began to seep through the tree cover. The lights of the village, the first stop on anyone's journey into the national park.

I was grateful that everyone picked up the pace. Finally, we broke through the woods into the village.

I released a nervous chuckle. "Please tell me sherpas don't do a lot of night hiking."

"Hardly ever," Rafe said, "but I felt something out there, too."

"If it was dangerous, it would have attacked," Connor said. "Probably just a rabbit or something."

"Whatever it was, it's gone now," Lucas said. "And we're supposed to be in our beds."

Connor and Rafe headed for their cabin. But Lucas hesitated. Finally he said, "Happy birthday, Kayla."

"Oh, thanks." His words were almost as surprising as the party.

He looked as though he wanted to say something else. Instead, he shoved his hands into the pockets of his jeans and walked off. I wasn't quite sure what to make of that.

Lindsey, Brittany, and I went to our cabin. As we were getting ready for bed, I said, "I can't believe you threw me a surprise party."

"You should have seen your face," Lindsey said. "You

were totally shocked."

"I can't believe you managed to keep it a secret."

She smiled brightly. "Believe me, it wasn't easy."

After we were in bed and the lights were out, Lindsey whispered, "Hey, Kayla? So what did you wish for?"

My cheeks grew warm. "If I tell, it won't come true."

I wasn't really sure I wanted it to come true. I didn't know what had possessed me to make the wish I had. It haunted me now as I remembered the words that had run through my mind with such conviction.

I wish Lucas would kiss me.

TWO

I was crouched in a tiny, dark place. I was small, a kid. I had my hands pressed against my mouth so I wouldn't make a sound. I knew that if I made any noise they'd find me. I didn't want them to find me. Tears ran down my face. I was trembling.

They were out there. Bad things were out there. So I hid in the dark. No one could find me in the dark. No one would find me here.

Then I saw the light, coming closer and closer. The monster grabbed me—

I woke up screaming and flailing my arms. I hit something and screamed again.

"Hey, it's just me," Lindsey said.

The lamp on the table beside my bed came on. It was still dark outside. Lindsey was standing between my bed and hers, a look of horror on her face. "What the *hell*?" she asked.

I swiped away my tears. "Sorry, bad dream."

"No kidding."

Brittany was sitting up in bed staring at me as if I was the monster that crept through my nightmares. "You sounded like you were being murdered."

I shook my head. "Not me. My parents. It's a long story—" I hesitated.

"It's okay. It's private. I understand," Brittany said.

I was relieved by her acceptance of my need not to explain.

Lindsey sat on my bed, took me in her arms, and held me tightly. She knew my story. I'd confessed it all to her during the past year, as our friendship had strengthened.

"Are you going to be okay taking these campers out tomorrow?" Lindsey asked. "We could get out of this, wait for the next group."

"No." Shaking my head, I pulled away from her. "I have to face my fears, and going into the wilderness is part of that. I'll be okay. Tonight . . . I don't know, maybe it's because we were creeping through the woods. I haven't had a nightmare in a while."

"Just remember that we're here for you." She glanced back at Brittany.

Brittany nodded. "Yeah, we are. Sherpas stick together."

"Thanks." I released a deep sigh.

Lindsey moved to her bed. "Do you want me to leave the light on?"

"No, I'm fine now." Or as fine as I could be, considering my issues. The really strange thing was this unexplained fear that I was experiencing lately. It was like a foreshadowing or something—a deep-down sense that something I couldn't explain was going to happen.

Lindsey turned off the light, and I snuggled beneath the blankets. I wished I understood what was bothering me. My adoptive parents couldn't explain it. My shrink couldn't figure it out. But since I'd returned to the national park, whatever it was seemed stronger than before. Part of me wondered if it was somehow tied to what had happened to my parents.

Was something in my subconscious on the verge of breaking free? And if it did, how would my life change?

The next morning when I woke up, the lingering effects of the dream were still haunting me. The unpleasantness of it hung around like cobwebs that couldn't be brushed off. I forced myself to concentrate on something else.

My birthday.

I didn't feel any older. For some reason, I'd thought I'd feel more sophisticated, better able to flirt with guys, when I turned seventeen. Instead, I felt like the same old me.

Faint light was visible through the curtain. Dawn was well on its way to arriving. My first day as a sherpa with an actual assignment. I was about to embark on my maiden adventure of the summer. I couldn't wait.

The past week I'd been going through all kinds of preparation and training. This initial excursion would be my test. I reached over and turned on the lamp. Lindsey groaned and stuck her head under the pillow, mumbling something that sounded like *Go away*.

"Don't mind her," Brittany said as she got out of bed and then dropped to the floor and started doing push-ups. "She'd stay in bed all day if she had her way."

"I thought she enjoyed the woods."

"Thought wrong." She jumped to her feet and stretched. "She likes the woods well enough, but she'd rather not be here."

I glanced over at Lindsey. She'd never told me that. "So why is she?"

"It's expected. If you grow up around here, you're destined to be a sherpa during the summer."

"And you *all* grew up around here?"

"In Tarrant, just up the road."

You have to pass through it to get to the park. It looks like any other small town in America. "So in our little group, you're all friends?"

"Pretty much, yeah. Connor, Rafe, and Lucas left for college this past year. Lindsey and I have one more year in high school. Then we'll head out, too."

"Guess everyone can't wait to get away from home."

"Isn't that why you're here?"

I nodded. But there was more to it. I'd always enjoyed camping, but lately all I wanted to do was be in the outdoors. "I guess I should feel like an outsider here, but I don't."

She shrugged. "You're one of us, aren't you?"

I smiled at the thought of all the training I'd passed. "I'm most definitely a sherpa."

She angled her head and gave me a funny look that I couldn't quite interpret. Where was my shrink when I needed him? "Exactly," she said, but I had the feeling she'd wanted to say something else. "Dibs on the shower."

I watched her walk into the bathroom. She was really toned. I found it a little intimidating. I was all of five-foot-four, with a slender build. I hoped that hauling a pack and hiking all summer would add some muscle to my shape.

"Are you ready for your first official day as a sherpa?"

Lindsey asked as she sat up and ran her fingers through her white-blond hair.

I moved to the edge of the bed. "Honestly? I'm terrified."

She gave me an incredulous look. "Why? You aced all the training."

"Yeah, but that was all in a controlled environment. I know things can get hairy out in the real world."

"You're going to do great."

"Can I be honest with you?"

"Sure. Always."

"I'm a little worried because I'm assigned to Lucas's group. He sort of scares me. He's so intense."

"Don't let him get to you. All the guys feel like they have something to prove. When they were young, their dads were sherpas. So it's a tradition passed down from father to son. They've only let girls be sherpas for a few years now."

"Really?"

"Yeah. They didn't think girls were strong enough."

"Is that the reason Brittany starts her morning with push-ups?"

Lindsey rolled her eyes. "Yeah. Maybe she feels like she has something to prove, too. I don't take it nearly as seriously as everyone else does."

Brittany came out of the bathroom. Her long, dark

hair was pulled back severely into a tight braid. She was wearing cargo shorts, boots, and a red tank. She looked at her watch. "You know we have to report in about ten minutes."

"Oh my God." I rushed into the bathroom.

I wanted to take my time with the shower, keeping the water as hot as I could stand it, because I knew it would be my last one for many days. But I was pressed for time. No makeup would be needed on the trail, although I did use sunscreen—to try to keep my freckles at a minimum—and mascara. My eyelashes are a faint red, and without a touch of mascara they are barely visible. I slipped on my cargo pants, boots, and a thin tank top. Over the tank, I zipped a snug hoodie. I tied a bandana over my wild red hair.

I finished up my morning ritual by touching the pewter necklace I always wore. It was a circle of knots and twisted strands. Someone had once told me that it was a Celtic symbol for *guardian*. It seemed appropriate. It had belonged to my mother, and sometimes it made me feel as though she was watching over me.

When I stepped out of the bathroom, Brittany was gone and Lindsey was dressed in cargo shorts and a spaghetti-strap tank. She'd pulled her blond hair back into a pony-tail. She helped me adjust my pack onto my back and shoulders.

"If it gets too heavy, say something to Lucas," she

told me. "He can shift some of the supplies to the other guys."

"I'm not a weakling. I can carry my own stuff." I was a little insulted that she thought I'd need help.

"I'm just saying. Sherpas carried a lot of your stuff last summer, so you might not be used to all the weight."

"But this year, *I'm* a sherpa."

"Looks like you'll be a stubborn one, too," she mumbled.

I wasn't stubborn, but I was determined to pull my weight. And not to miss my adoptive parents. It was hard, though. Don't get me wrong, I loved my natural parents, but they'd been gone a long time. My adoptive parents had always treated me like I was their birth kid. I loved them with a fierceness that surprised me sometimes. But it was my nature to have strong emotions about things, at least according to my shrink. It was the reason that I was still coping with the senseless death of my parents.

I shivered as I stepped out of the cabin into the cool dawn air. The campers and guides were gathered in the center of the small village. The village was nestled just inside the national park. It housed the ranger station, a small first aid station, a gift shop, a camping supply store, and a tiny café. It was the last chance to stock up before heading out.

Excitement—and a little bit of nervousness—thrummed

through my veins. After all, I'd be responsible for the welfare of these campers.

Lindsey shut the cabin door behind me and knocked her shoulder against mine. "This is it, girlfriend. You ready?"

I took a deep breath. "I think so."

"You're going to have way more fun this summer than you did last year."

I adjusted my pack, took a deep breath, and strode toward the group that had gathered. Dr. Keane, his son, and several grad students would be hiking into the wilderness. Six sherpas would be traveling with them. That was a lot for such a small group, but Dr. Keane had special equipment that he needed for whatever it was he was trying to teach his students, so he'd hired more of us. Which was fine with me, since I was still learning. Having someone to cover my back sounded like a great idea. I didn't want to be the one responsible for making a decision that would put us all on the nightly news.

One guy stepped away from the group. "Hey, Kayla," he called out with a bright smile as he approached me.

Lindsey just gave me a questioning raise of her eyebrow and continued on while I stopped to talk with Mason. He was not only one of Dr. Keane's students, but also his son. I'd met him the day before. He was really cute. His dark-brown hair fell over his brow and covered his left eye.

"Hey, yourself," I said.

"I was afraid you weren't going to make it."

He had so much energy that it bolstered my own excitement about the coming adventure. "No, just off to a late start."

"This trip is going to be so awesome," he said.

"Have you done much backcountry hiking?"

"Oh yeah. Not here, of course. But Dad and I have gone through other national forests. We've also done a lot of hiking in Europe."

"So you and your dad are close?"

He shrugged. "Sometimes. I mean he's still a parent, you know? And my grad school advisor. Plus he treats me like I'm a kid."

I smiled in commiseration. "Tell me about it."

"Maybe I will. Later tonight." He looked down as though suddenly uncomfortable. His stance reminded me of Rick—the guy who'd taken me to the junior prom— right before he'd asked me to go with him. As though he was gathering his courage, afraid he'd get rejected.

"We're going to have a blast," I assured Mason, not sure why I was encouraging him when I'd only be with him for a few days. Except that he was cute and seemed friendly. And there weren't any rules against getting involved with the campers. When you're out in the woods together for several days or weeks, things were certain to develop.

Lifting his eyes to mine, he gave me a big smile. He had eyes the color of clover. With his tawny skin and dark hair, they really stood out.

"Maybe we could walk together." He said it like he wasn't sure if he should make it a real suggestion, a statement, or simply an inquiry.

"I'd like—"

"City Girl, you're with me."

Okay, I didn't know why I knew that order was directed at me. No one had ever called me *City Girl*. Maybe it was because I recognized the voice. Or maybe it was simply the nearness of it. To be singled out irritated but thrilled me at the same time. I worked to get all my emotions under control while I slowly turned to face Lucas. "Excuse me? 'City Girl'?"

"You're from the city, right?"

"Yeah, I suppose *Dallas* could be called a city. And why do I have to hike with you?"

He shifted the weight of his pack on his shoulders. It was twice the size of mine. I would have been bent over, but he stood straight as though it was nothing. "Because you're new and I need to check your skills. We'll take the lead."

He was dressed in cargo shorts and a black T-shirt. His hair was straight and lanky, but the variety of colors made it look anything except boring. His silver eyes held a challenge. Yeah, I was new, but I wasn't stupid enough to argue against an order before we'd even gotten started. He could easily declare me too much trouble and leave me here. I resented that he had so much power and wasn't afraid to wield it. I had a problem with authority, obviously.

I gave him a sarcastic salute. To my stunned surprise, his lips twitched as though he were fighting back a smile. Wasn't that fascinating?

"Interesting necklace. It's a Celtic symbol for *guardian*," he said quietly.

I couldn't have been more surprised if he'd suddenly started talking about designer clothes. He didn't strike me as someone who'd care about Celtic anything. I touched it. "Yeah, that's what I heard. It belonged to my mom."

"Makes it special."

His eyes held mine, and it was as though we were the only two people around. For a moment, he wasn't my boss. He was just the guy I'd met last summer, the guy I'd dreamed about way too many times to count. I didn't know why he haunted my dreams, my thoughts. I didn't know why I wanted to confess about the wish I'd made the night before. Didn't know why I wanted to kiss him so badly. His gaze dropped to my lips as though maybe he was thinking the same thing I was.

Suddenly he seemed irritated with himself, maybe

because Mason wasn't even trying to hide the fact that he was studying us with curiosity.

"Meet me at the front in five," Lucas suddenly barked. Then he gave Mason an unfriendly once-over. "Be sure you stay close to a guide, Mason. Wouldn't want you to get lost."

Mason's green eyes narrowed as he watched Lucas until he disappeared. The dislike was shimmering off him in waves. I wasn't usually so attuned to people, but something about being in the woods brought out my primal instincts, I guessed. Maybe it was the whole getting-back-to-nature thing. But there was definitely some tension between these two.

"Who put him in charge?" Mason groused.

"The park rangers, I think. He's supposed to be really good. I heard he found a family that got lost last summer when no one else could."

"Really? How'd he manage that?"

"Followed their tracks or something. You'll have to ask him."

"Yeah, like he'd tell me anything."

"Did you get into it with him or something?"

"Not yet, but I wouldn't be surprised if we do. Something about the guy seems off."

Mason didn't strike me as a fighter. Lucas would obviously kick his ass, but I didn't think Mason would appreciate my assessment of his fighting skills. Apparently I wasn't the only one feeling animalistic today.

"He's not really worth the bother," I said.

Mason snapped his head around and gave me a strange smile. "You don't think I can beat him."

"He's got the whole working-out thing going."

"Don't let my love of academics fool you. I can hold my own in a fight."

"I've no doubt." It was the only thing I could say. I didn't think a fight was in the best interest of our goal. "Anyway, I'd better go."

He touched my hand just for a second. "Uh, I've got something for you." He reached into his pocket, brought out a small package, and extended it toward me. "Happy birthday."

I looked at him with surprise. "How did you know?"

His cheeks turned red. "Last night, I couldn't sleep. I was out walking. Saw the party."

Had he been following us? Was he what I'd heard? "Why didn't you say something, join us?"

"I'm not a party crasher. Open it."

I did. Inside was a braided leather bracelet. "Oh, thanks. I like it." I beamed at him.

He appeared even more embarrassed. "There's not much to choose from in the stores around here. Most of it is camping stuff and cheap souvenirs."

"It's awesome," I reassured him, just before I slipped it onto my wrist.

"So maybe we can get together later," he said.

It wasn't like we'd get together later and go on a date. We were pretty much limited to group outings, but still we could have some fun. "Yeah, definitely."

Then I went to catch up with Lucas. Day one and I was already confused about a lot of things: my attraction to Lucas and my interest in Mason. Mason was definitely the safer of the two. The question was: Did I want safe?

THREE

I caught up with Lucas a couple of minutes later. I didn't show him the gift from Mason, and part of me hoped he wouldn't notice it. I didn't know why, but I didn't think he'd approve.

"Mason was out in the woods last night," I told him. "I think he's who I heard."

"I know he was in the woods. I smelled him."

"Excuse me?"

"That soap he uses—strong stuff. Anyway, I don't think he's who I felt watching us."

"But he told me that he watched."

"Maybe it was him, then."

I knew a brush-off when I heard it. "You don't sound convinced."

"I just think we need to stay alert."

I nodded. "Okay."

"Let's go!" he called out to our group.

When Lucas said that we'd take the lead, apparently he'd meant *he* would take the lead and I would follow closely behind. I told myself that we had no choice except to go single file because the trail was narrow. Today we were following a path that others had taken enough times so it was clearly marked and the brush didn't encroach, but I knew at some point we'd diverge into an area no one else had explored. That was my favorite part of backwoods hiking—going where no one had gone before. It was always an adventure, with a surprise around every corner. And right now, the biggest surprise was Lucas and how much I enjoyed watching his movements. He was confident and sure-footed.

I knew he was attending a university somewhere and had just returned to work for the summer, but that was about it. What I knew about him wasn't enough to cover the needle of my compass.

I did know he was in amazing shape. He was barely breathing, while my breaths—to my complete mortification—were taking on a labored quality. The path was at an incline and the rugged forest terrain was mountainous.

Traveling over it was a workout. I'd thought I was in shape. *Ha!*

"Just a little farther," Lucas finally said.

I was mortified that he not only heard me gasping, but felt obligated to let me know that he noticed me struggling. While no one had made me feel like I was an outsider, I knew the truth: I was. "I'm fine."

He glanced back without altering his stride. "But the prof and his students are suffering."

I thought of his apparent dislike for Mason—or Mason's for him. "Are you trying to prove something to them?"

"If I were, I wouldn't stop at all."

Yeah, he could probably go all day without taking a break. I felt a strange mixture of admiration and jealousy. I had no idea why I cared, but I wanted to be his equal, wanted him to be impressed with my stamina. Wanted him to be impressed with *me*.

The path widened just a bit. He slowed his stride until we were walking side by side.

"So how long have you been a sherpa?" I asked.

He shifted his silver gaze over to me. "Four years."

"Is that the reason they put me on your team? Because you're so experienced?"

He seemed to study me in that still way he had, before he said, "I requested you."

My jaw dropped, but I didn't think he had time to notice, because at the same time I tripped over my own feet. Lucas moved with a swiftness that astounded me, catching me and steadying me before I fell beneath the weight of my pack. His large, warm hands gripped my arms.

I should have been mortified by my clumsiness, but I wasn't really thinking about it. I was intrigued by what he'd said.

"Why?" I asked. "Why request me?"

"Because I didn't think anyone else could protect you as well as I could."

"So you're what? Supersherpa? And you think I'm not capable of taking care of myself?"

"I'm not the one who just tripped."

I decided it would sound stupid to argue that I'd tripped because of his words, that my clumsiness was somehow his fault.

"Are we stopping here?" Lindsey asked, as she approached and gave me an odd look.

"Yeah," Lucas said. He released his hold on me, stepped away, and shucked off his backpack with the ease of someone removing a jacket. He leaned it up against a tree. I worked my way out of mine and did the same.

"We'll take fifteen. Be sure to hydrate," Lucas said when everyone else had caught up with us. "I'm going to scout the area ahead."

Before anyone could respond, he disappeared between two trees.

Okay, Mr. I-can-leave-you-all-in-the-dust, I thought. *Be that way. Prove you're not human, that you don't need to rest.*

"Doesn't that guy ever get tired?" Mason asked grumpily as he dropped to the ground after removing his backpack.

"They say he's the best," Dr. Keane said. His hair was dark, peppered with white. Even in his hiking clothes he looked distinguished, as though at any moment he'd break into a lecture. He didn't seem the type to have an Indiana Jones mode. He strolled over to two of his students—Tyler and Ethan—who were carrying a large wooden crate on a litter, huffing heavily and sweating profusely. He helped them get the crate safely to the ground.

"What is that stuff, Professor?" Connor asked.

"Just some equipment we'll use to collect samples once we get farther into the wilderness."

"You must be planning to collect a lot of samples."

Dr. Keane smiled in a way that reminded me of my therapist when he was letting me know that he knew things my feeble mind would never dream of. "I intend to get my money's worth out of this trip. And I only brought students with avid curiosities, so I'm sure there is much out here that they'll want to examine closely."

So Mason wasn't the only one with resentment issues. I had no idea what the park charged for the use of sherpas. I only knew that I was paid minimum wage. The thought was that our real reward was being able to spend our summer in the wilds. We wouldn't be here if we didn't love what we were doing.

The other grad students—David, Jon, and Monique—sat together in a cluster, while the sherpas mingled together. David and Jon seemed a little old to be grad students. I wondered if they'd decided later in life what they wanted to do. I thought they were probably close to thirty. Monique was supermodel-lithe and lovely. She was tall with milk-chocolate skin and a flawless complexion.

Considering Dr. Keane's attitude about getting his money's worth, I didn't think it was a good idea for us to separate ourselves into separate camps: sherpas versus grad students. I dug a water bottle out of my backpack and sat beside Mason. He was picking at his thumbnail.

"What happened?" I asked.

"Oh, chipped it when we were packing supplies this morning. It keeps catching on things."

"I have a nail file you can use." I unzipped the pocket on my backpack.

"You brought a file?" He was truly astounded.

"Sure. No girl with any respect for her manicure

travels in the wilds without a nail file."

Laughing, he took my offering and smoothed out his nail before handing the file back to me. I put it back into my pack.

"You need to be drinking," I reminded him.

"Oh yeah, right." He grabbed a bottle from his backpack and guzzled for a few seconds. Then he peered over at me. "What do you know about that guy?"

"What guy?"

"The guy who thinks he's in charge."

"If you're referring to Lucas, he *is* in charge. Has papers and everything to prove it." I wasn't sure why I was defending his superior behavior.

"Whatever. Is he from around here?"

"Yeah. I mean, I think he goes to college somewhere else but he grew up around here."

"Weird hair. I mean, who has hair that's all different colors?"

I sort of liked it, but I didn't defend it because I didn't want anyone thinking I had a thing for Lucas. I wasn't quite sure how to define what I felt for him. On the one hand, he was incredibly hot. On the other hand, he was older and seemed way more experienced than I was. The truth was, he intimidated me a little.

"So what about you?" Mason asked, interrupting my strange musings. "I overheard you say you were from

45

Dallas. This place is practically near Canada. What made you decide to work so far from home?"

My gut said to give a flippant answer, but the whole key to effective therapy was facing my past and not hiding from it. Besides, I was still having some residual creepy feelings from the nightmare. Maybe I needed to unburden, and Mason seemed like a nice guy, someone who was interested in me anyway. I touched the braided leather he'd given me and said as quietly as I could, "My shrink recommended it."

"You go to a shrink?"

I couldn't tell if he was impressed or appalled. The kids at my school tended to think if anyone went to a psychiatrist, she was on the verge of going on a killing spree, so I never talked about it with anyone. At home I was much more closed off within myself than I was here in the wild. I felt more at home here than I did in Dallas. Given a choice between living in the city or in the forest, I'd choose the forest every time. Suddenly I felt a need to connect with someone on a level I never had reached before. I nodded at Mason and admitted, "Yeah."

"So what—you're bipolar or something?"

Okay, there it was—the negative connotation all wrapped up with a little bow. "Let's just say I have issues." And because he'd hit a sore spot, I continued tartly, "My parents were killed in these woods. My therapist says I need to embrace this forest in order to get past them dying here."

"Wow, that's some heavy shit."

Obviously he had a problem discussing emotional matters, and whatever connection I thought I'd felt with him earlier had been totally misguided. Already I regretted opening up to him. "Yeah. I don't usually tell people that. Forget I mentioned it. I don't know why I told you."

"No, hey, my bad. I've never known anyone whose parents were killed. I mean, I just wasn't expecting that. How were they killed? Wild animals?"

I shook my head. "I'm sorry. I don't want to talk about it anymore. I shouldn't have even brought it up."

"Hey, it's okay. Not that they died, but that you don't want to talk about it. From the moment we met yesterday, I've kinda felt this connection with you. Really, if you want to talk, I'm here."

I gave him a hesitant smile. "Thanks."

"Sure. Besides, I'm safe, you know? You'll just see me for a couple of weeks and then I'll go away. Unless . . ." His voice trailed off.

"Unless what?" I prodded.

"Unless we get really tight on this trip. Then who knows? With email and text messaging, long-distance relationships can work."

Whip out the engagement ring already. "Whoa, you move fast."

"Just throwing out possibilities." He leaned toward me. "I'm definitely interested in possibilities."

I was, too. Or I thought I was. So why didn't I give him a wink and nudge him in the right direction? Why did I find myself glancing around as though I were doing something wrong? And why did I nearly come out of my skin when I saw Lucas leaning against a tree watching me?

What was with this guy and his constant lurking at the edge of the group? And why in the world was I wondering what sort of possibilities *he* might hold?

"We need to head out if we want to make our designated camp by dark," Lucas suddenly announced. "City Girl, you're still with me."

As a rule, I'm a team player—except when I'm not. I was still close enough to the village that he might send me back if I staged a mutiny. After tripping earlier, I couldn't even argue that I didn't need watching.

I grabbed my backpack, shrugged it on, and trudged over to him. "Is it really necessary for me to walk in your shadow?"

"For now." He jerked his head toward something behind me. "Did you want to walk with *him*?"

I knew he was referring to Mason. "Maybe. What does it matter to you?"

"You get into trouble and all you'll see is his butt as he runs off to ensure his own safety."

"You don't know that."

"I'm a good judge of people. Mason is all bark and no bite."

"And I guess you're all bite."

A corner of his mouth hitched up in what might have been a smile. "Depends on whether or not someone needs biting."

Before I could respond with something clever, his version of a smile disappeared and he said, "There could be danger out there. Stick with me for a while longer."

He was talking to *me* about danger? Did he not know my history? Why did he care anyway? Because I was the newbie? Or was there more to it? And why did I want there to be more? I considered arguing further, but everyone had gathered around and I was the holdup.

I shrugged—as much as I was able to shrug with a two-ton backpack on my shoulders. "Let's go, Boss."

FOUR

"Werewolves? You really believe in the existence of werewolves?" I nearly strangled myself holding back my laughter as I asked the question. While I knew that in retail the customer was always right, I didn't know if this mantra applied to the campers who had hired me to serve as a guide. In this case, they were definitely wrong, and I just couldn't be silent about it.

Several of us were sitting by the campfire with Dr. Keane. The rest of our day had gone pretty much like that morning: trudging through the forest, stopping for a break, trudging on. Until we'd reached this large clearing and Lucas had announced we'd set up camp here. It had been dusk by then. Now it was night and we were toasting marshmallows. Cliché, but oh, they were good.

Dr. Keane had been regaling us with ancient tales about werewolves, which had been fascinating—absurd, but fascinating—and then he'd segued into talking about wolves spotted in the wilderness around here. Wolves he was convinced were, in reality, werewolves. He believed this particular national forest was their hunting ground, where they hid away from the real world.

"Why is that so hard to believe?" Dr. Keane asked now, in answer to my question. He was sitting on a little folding stool, looking very professorial. All he needed was a red bow tie. "Every culture has a legend about man shifting into an animal shape. Legends are rooted in fact."

"I'm with Kayla on this one," Lindsey said, sitting beside Connor. "Werewolves exist only in fiction. Look at Big Foot and the Loch Ness Monster. They've all been debunked."

"I don't know," Connor said. "Dr. Keane could be onto something here. There was a guy in my dorm that could have been a werewolf. He never shaved, cut his hair, or bathed. It was hard to call him human."

I bit back more laughter. Apparently none of us were taking his theories seriously.

"But what if it *is* true? That werewolves exist and they inhabit this forest?" Mason asked. He was sitting on a

51

log beside me. He was very particular about his marsh-mallows, toasting them slowly and carefully to a golden brown. On a good day, I didn't have that much patience. Tonight I was so tired that I had none at all. My marsh-mallows were quickly poked into the fire and tossed into my mouth.

"Then we're all doomed to die," I quipped in an evil horror-movie scientist kind of way. All I needed was a flash of lightning and a boom of thunder for effect.

Connor and Lindsey chuckled at my theatrical display. The prof's students even smiled.

"Or we all turn into werewolves," Lucas said ominously. He wasn't sitting in our circle, but was leaning against a tree. "Isn't that how it works, Professor? A werewolf bites you and then you become one?"

"That's one possibility. The other is that it's genetic. Werewolves are born with some sort of genetic mutation—"

"What? Like in *X-Men*?" Lucas interrupted with a smirk.

"Even fiction has an element of truth in it," Dr. Keane insisted.

"But why are the werewolves the 'mutations'?" Lucas made little quote marks in the air. "What if everyone else is the real mutation? Maybe we all started out as werewolves."

"Interesting theory, but if that were the case, they'd be

the dominant species, don't you think? They'd be hunting us instead of us hunting them."

"We're *hunting* them?" Rafe challenged.

"I gave the wrong impression," Dr. Keane said. "Discovering them is what I was referring to."

"If they don't want to be *discovered*, maybe they'll come after us," Brittany said. "What then?"

"I don't think we have anything to worry about tonight," Lucas said, glancing up at the sky. "No full moon."

"That works only if the transformation is lunar controlled," Dr. Keane said. "What if they could transform at will?"

"Then I'd say we're in big trouble." His delivery was deadpan, and I wasn't sure if he was serious or teasing.

"*You're* not buying into this, are you?" I asked. Lucas was the last one I thought would swallow this ridiculous notion of werewolves.

He winked at me and my heart gave a little tug. "Just know that when I zip up my tent tonight, I'm not leaving it until morning."

"Tents won't stop a werewolf," Mason said, before blowing on his perfect marshmallow.

"There's never been a documented account of a healthy wolf attacking a human," Lucas challenged him.

"We're not talking wolves, dude," Mason said sharply, turning to glare at Lucas. When he did, his stick took a dip and his gooey marshmallow landed in the dirt. I didn't know why that bothered me. All that work for nothing, maybe. "We're talking *werewolves*. A person who turns into a beast. They're out there, and we're going to prove it."

And earlier you questioned my *being in therapy?*

"Is that what this expedition is about?" Lucas asked in a deadly calm voice that sent a shiver racing up my spine.

"Mason is just a little overzealous," Dr. Keane said. "We are hoping to see some wolves and perhaps study them. I'll admit to being fascinated by the notion of lycanthropy. Do I truly believe it exists? No, of course not, but I like to be open-minded enough to leave room for the possibility."

"Wolves were extinct in this area until about twenty years ago, when a few were brought in to repopulate the area. The original wolves have probably died off by now, but their descendents have flourished. They're a protected species," Lucas said.

"We're not going to harm them," Dr. Keane assured Lucas.

"Well, then, maybe you'll get lucky and see some." Lucas shoved away from the tree. "We've got an early start tomorrow. I'm going to bed. Rafe, make sure everything is secure for the night."

"You got it," Rafe said, before popping a burned marshmallow into his mouth.

Once Lucas had gone into his tent, the tension around the campfire eased. I had a feeling I wasn't the only one who thought Lucas and Mason were headed toward a brawl.

"Do you really believe in all that stuff?" I asked Mason.

Chuckling, he shook his head. "Nah, but wouldn't it be cool?"

"They're always a little rabid in the movies," I reminded him.

"A wolf bit me once," he announced.

"Seriously?"

"Yeah." He leaned down and rolled up his pants leg. There on his calf was a horrible scar. "Took a chunk."

"Mason has been studying wolves ever since," Dr. Keane said, his voice echoing a sense of pride.

"But Lucas said there were no documented accounts of wolf attacks."

"Guess he doesn't know everything," Mason said quietly, and it sent a shiver through me.

"So do you turn into a werewolf when there's a full moon?" Lindsey asked.

Mason snorted. "I wish."

"I always root for the werewolves," Lindsey replied.

"They get such a bad rap in movies. Demons from hell. I think they're a metaphor for how badly we treat people who are different."

"It's just fiction, Lindsey," Connor said. "No subliminal messages or great truths revealed. And anyway, a girl isn't going to scream and snuggle up against you if you're watching a movie where the werewolf is sweet and understanding."

"But there's a bias against them. They're always the bad guy. Just once, I'd like to see a werewolf portrayed as heroic."

"You really take it personally," Mason said, starting to toast his next marshmallow.

"What can I say? I like canines."

"Vampires get the same bad rap," Brittany said. "Are you going to defend them?"

"There are lots of vampires who are portrayed in movies as fighting their addiction to blood, trying to be noble. I'm just saying it would be nice to see a noble werewolf in a movie once in a while."

"They always lose their humanity when they transform," Mason said distractedly. He removed his perfect marshmallow from the fire and glanced around. "Or at least that's the way it is in the movies."

"In all the legends, werewolves do horrible, unforgivable things," Dr. Keane said. "It's only natural that Hollywood would incorporate those fears in its storytelling."

"Still," Lindsey mumbled, but she seemed to have given up arguing on behalf of werewolves. It was silly anyway. It was, after all, only make-believe.

Mason offered me his lightly browned marshmallow. "I can't take it," I told him. "You worked too hard to get it just right."

"Because I wanted it perfect for you."

How could I refuse? I popped it into my mouth. It was heavenly. I smiled at him. He smiled back. When we weren't discussing werewolves—and Lucas wasn't around—I enjoyed being with Mason. And he was safe. He didn't make me want to do things I shouldn't do—things that went way beyond a kiss.

After Brittany, Lindsey, and I got into our tent, Brittany stretched out on her sleeping bag, rolled over, and went to sleep without a word. I quirked an eyebrow at Lindsey. She shrugged. "Something is bothering her. I don't know what."

We got into our own sleeping bags. Lindsey turned out our main lantern and turned on a small penlight. It cast a ghostly glow.

"So what's up with you and Mason?" she asked quietly.

"I'm not sure. I mean, I like him."

"You need to be careful. Some guys think that sherpas are only for hooking up—that we're easy."

"I don't think Mason's like that. And I'm definitely not easy."

"Just be careful. I don't want to see you get hurt on your first expedition."

"I might hang out with him, but I would never get serious with someone I may never see again."

"Yeah, that's what they all say," Brittany muttered.

"Thought you were asleep," Lindsey said.

"How can I sleep with you two yammering?"

Lindsey stuck out her tongue at Brittany's back. I stifled a giggle. Lindsey settled down into her bag. "Just be careful," she whispered before curling up to go to sleep.

I stared at the tent ceiling. Lindsey wanted the penlight on to serve as our nightlight. I'd learned last summer when we were out in the wilds that she wasn't a big fan of absolute darkness. Late at night, after my parents went to sleep, I'd snuck out and crawled into Lindsey's tent. We'd talked for hours about school, clothes, and guys. She was the first person outside of my family who I'd ever told about my parents getting killed. For some reason, except for last night, I didn't have the nightmares when I was around Lindsey—maybe because she didn't define me by my past. In some ways, she was far more accepting than my therapist.

I'd met Brittany last summer as well, but I didn't feel

as close to her. Maybe because I sensed that she had her own issues. She was snoring now. It was a little snuffle, similar to the sound my Lhasa at home, Fargo, made.

But it wasn't the light or the noise that was keeping me awake. It was wolves. They weren't howling, but I had a feeling they were lurking nearby. If what Lucas said was correct, they'd been in these woods for only twenty years. Long enough to have been around when my original parents and I had come camping that long-ago summer. Had those hunters seen them? Were we hiking now near where the wolves had been, near where my parents had died?

I hadn't wanted to visit the spot last summer. I wasn't ready for that. Besides, no one had seemed to remember where it had happened. Or so they had said. Maybe they were afraid the trauma would be too much for me. But tonight, I was remembering low-throated growling and snarling that weren't dream-induced. Had we been running from wolves? But Lucas had said they never attacked people, so my strange musings made no sense.

What had really happened that day?

I threw back the top of the sleeping bag and sat up. I suddenly felt as though I had to get out of the tent. I hadn't bothered to undress earlier, so all I had to do was put on my hiking boots. When they were securely tied, I grabbed my flashlight. As quietly as I could, I unzipped the tent opening and slipped outside.

A couple of lanterns had been left on, but no one was

around. I didn't want company. I just wanted . . .

I didn't know what I wanted.

Face your fears, Dr. Brandon had urged me. It would be a lot easier to do if I knew exactly what those fears were. I honestly didn't have a clue. I just had a sense that something momentous was on the horizon, that I was poised on the edge of change. I didn't know what to expect, but I felt as though it was connected to my past and would influence my future. I had questions, but no answers—fear without justification.

I skirted around the side of the tent and headed into the forest. I'd taken only a couple of steps before I heard low voices. They were nearby, near one of the other tents.

I knew it was none of my business, but I crept closer.

"I know, Dad. God, how many times do I have to say I'm sorry?" I recognized the voice. It was Mason.

"We don't want to raise any suspicions."

"You're the one who started talking about werewolves."

"As legend."

"But you were sounding like a preacher, preaching the gospel of werewolves. That's the reason Kayla asked you if you believed in them. You did just as much damage as I did."

"We just need to stay alert and be more careful about what we say to them."

"Like I said, I'm not the one who started it."

"Seriously, Mason, any of our guides could be one."

I had to put my hand over my mouth to stop myself from laughing out loud.

"My money's on Lucas," Mason said, and I was even more shocked. "That guy is too quiet. It's eerie how he can get so still. Why does he keep disappearing, every time we stop to rest? What does he do when he's gone?"

"We'll figure it out. Don't worry, we'll figure it out."

I stood there, stunned, while their voices got quieter as they walked away toward their tents. What were they saying? That they thought the sherpas were werewolves? That Lucas was a werewolf?

The whole idea of people morphing into animals was ludicrous, but the thought of anyone truly believing it was frightening. I thought about all the equipment they were carrying. Was there a cage inside that large crate? Were they going to try to capture a wolf? And when they realized the wolf was just a wolf . . . what then?

I knew people believed in all kinds of things that didn't exist, but this seemed a little out there.

As quietly and cautiously as possible, I crept toward the trees. I certainly didn't want them to hear me, to know that I'd overheard their conversation. I didn't think they'd kill me to silence me or anything crazy like that, but I was a little spooked that they seemed to be on a werewolf-hunting expedition. Although where was the real harm? People searched the skies for UFOs. Some believed they'd been probed by aliens or been in a spaceship. Others invested in fancy equipment to detect the existence of ghosts. I guessed it wasn't so strange that someone would believe in werewolves. I thought it was loony tunes, but as long as they didn't hurt anyone, I supposed they had as much right as anyone to explore the forest.

When I thought I was far enough away not to be detected, I switched on the flashlight. It provided a reassuring light, but strangely I was as comforted by the trees surrounding me as by anything else. I heard the leaves rustling in the breeze almost like a lullaby. For a crazy moment, I thought I could hear my mother singing. I didn't believe in ghosts, but I believed that the soul or the spirit or whatever made us who we were lived beyond death. So maybe believing in werewolves wasn't so crazy after all.

"Going somewhere, City Girl?"

I swung the beam of the flashlight around to where the voice originated. Lucas was standing beside me. I hadn't heard him approach. How had he arrived so quietly?

I pressed my hand to my chest, where my rapidly pounding heart was threatening to crack a rib. "You nearly gave me a heart attack." My voice held accusation—rightly so.

"What are you doing out here?" he asked.

"I couldn't sleep."

"So you thought it was a good idea to wander from camp?"

"I wasn't wandering. I was just—" Why was I explaining myself? I narrowed my eyes at him. "What are *you* doing out here?"

"Couldn't sleep either. What was keeping *you* awake?"

Having regretted being so open with Mason earlier, I decided to be vague. "Just a lot on my mind."

"Your parents were killed out here, right?"

His voice held sympathy and understanding.

"How did you know?" I asked.

"Heard something about it last summer. We were told why you were here. So we wouldn't say something insensitive when we were guiding you through the wilderness. Must have been hard coming back here."

I nodded, my throat suddenly thick with unshed tears. "Yeah."

"If you want to walk some more, I'll walk with you."

"Thanks, but . . . I'm not really in the mood for company."

"No talking. Just walking. I can keep an eye out, keep you safe."

"And if we get lost?"

"I know these woods like the back of my hand. When

you grow up in Tarrant, the national forest is your playground."

"Okay, yeah. If you don't mind. I just need to wander for a while." I started walking and he fell into step beside me. I didn't like to admit it, but he was way more comforting than the trees or the beam of my flashlight. It was actually kind of nice just having him there, not needing to keep up a conversation or anything.

It was strange, but as we walked along, I was able to smell the unique scent of his skin. It was an earthy smell like the woods around us. It was pleasant, powerful, and sexy. I couldn't believe how quiet he was. I swept my flashlight back for a second. He was barefoot.

"Isn't that a little dangerous?" I asked as I redirected my light forward.

"My feet are tough. I've gone barefoot since I was a kid."

"You move so quietly."

"Had to learn to do that. Connor, Rafe, and I used to play war games with the other kids. The only way to win was to be able to sneak up on people undetected."

"And you like to win."

"Absolutely. No point in playing if your goal is to lose."

I came to a stop and leaned my back against a tree. I pointed the flashlight down so we had light but our faces were lost in the shadows. But still I felt him watching me. "Do you have any bad memories?" I asked. He had an idea about mine. I wanted us on even ground.

"Everyone has some bad memories," he said.

"That's not an answer."

"Yeah, I've got some."

His voice held no emotion, and I knew he wasn't about to talk about them, but knowing that he had them was enough. I sighed heavily. "I was with them when they were killed. My parents. But I don't really remember what happened. I remember the echo of the gunshots. They were so loud. And then my parents were dead. It's been driving me crazy lately, ever since I came back to the forest this year. Last year it was like I was inside a bubble, trying to insulate myself from the past. I didn't want to face it. But this year it's different. It's as though something inside me wants to break free. I can't explain it, but I feel like I'm on the verge of remembering something really important."

He moved closer to me and skimmed his knuckles along my cheek. Until that moment, I didn't realize I was crying. I released a short burst of embarrassed laughter. "I'm sorry. I didn't mean to lay all that heavy stuff on you."

"That's okay. It has to be difficult, being back here again. I love these woods. You must hate them."

"You'd think I would, but I don't. In a way, when I'm

here, I feel a connection to my parents."

He kept silent. In an odd way, it made me think better of him for not trying to say something, because anything would have been trite. I felt like maybe I should pull away, but I didn't. Even if he felt my pain, he couldn't experience it.

"According to my therapist, I'm supposed to face what happened, but I just want to forget it. I get these nightmares . . . they make no sense."

His knuckles were touching my face again, but his thumb was stroking the curve of my cheek. It was incredibly soothing. Even in the darkness, his eyes held mine.

"Was it night or day?" he asked quietly.

"Night. But just barely. The tail end of dusk. Light enough to see, but not to see everything. Not yet dark enough for a flashlight."

"You were all together?"

"Yeah, they wanted to show me something. We'd left the others." I blinked and tried to draw up the memory. "I'd forgotten there were others." *Who were they? Family? No, they would have taken me in. Friends?* I shook my head. "I don't know who they were. Do you think it's important?"

"I'm not a shrink. What did your parents want to show you?"

"I can't remember. I was scared about something. I'd

seen something. I don't know."

"I wouldn't worry about it. If it's important, it'll come to you."

"I thought you weren't a shrink."

"I'm not, but I know that sometimes trying too hard is worse than not trying at all."

"That makes no sense."

His teeth flashed white in the darkness. I almost pointed my flashlight up, just to see that smile for real. Out here, away from everyone else, when he wasn't the leader, when he was just a guy, he wasn't nearly as intimidating.

"So why couldn't you sleep?" I asked. Assuming his earlier answer hadn't simply been a mocking repeat of mine.

"All that talk about werewolves. Had me shaking in my hiking boots."

He made me smile. "Yeah, right. You're afraid of the big, bad werewolf."

He grinned. He had an incredibly sexy grin.

"They think you're a werewolf," I said and went on to explain, "Dr. Keane and Mason."

"Do they?" I heard the amusement in his voice.

"You think it's funny."

"As long as they're not carrying silver bullets."

"Oh, great. You truly believe all that stuff, too?"

"No, but I don't want them shooting at any wolves we

might happen to come across."

"You're protective of them."

"I've spent a lot of time in these woods. You get to know the animals. I don't want to see them hurt. Just like I wouldn't want to see you hurt."

He lowered his head just a little and I had this incredible realization that he was going to kiss me. Not only that—I desperately wanted him to.

A sudden howling in the distance made us both go still. It was a lonely sound. For some strange reason, it made me think of an animal in mourning.

"We should probably head back," Lucas said quietly, putting distance between us.

I nodded. "Yeah."

I directed the flashlight toward the path.

"Actually, it's this way," Lucas said, taking my hand and guiding me in the right direction.

"Are you sure?"

"Positive."

I wasn't sure how I'd gotten turned around, but I followed his lead. Soon, I could see the dim lights of our campsite.

"Thanks for going with me," I said when I got to my tent.

"Any time you need to go for a walk at night, just let me know. It's not safe to go out alone."

It wasn't until I was curled back into my sleeping bag that I recalled he'd been out there alone. Why was it safe for him and not for me?

Then I heard another howling wolf. This one was much closer, so close that I could have sworn it was just outside our tent. I thought I should have been afraid. Instead, just like when I'd been walking with Lucas, I felt comforted.

After I drifted off to sleep, for the first time in a long time, when I dreamed about wolves I didn't wake up screaming.

FIVE

The next day was pretty much like the day before except that the terrain became rougher. Everyone struggled a little more. Everyone except the sherpas. At one point, Lucas suggested that Connor and Rafe carry the crate, but Tyler and Ethan insisted they could take care of it.

"Wonder what's inside that they're so protective of?" Brittany asked.

After we'd stopped for lunch, Lucas hadn't insisted that I stay near the front, so I'd moved back to hike with Brittany and Lindsey.

"I bet I can get them to tell me," Lindsey said.

"I think maybe it's a cage," I murmured.

"A cage? For what?" Brittany asked.

In the light of day, I felt silly saying it. "I overheard them last night after the campfire. I think they really believe werewolves are out here."

Lindsey snorted. "They're not the first. We always get some campers who hear the rumors and think they can find the evidence. And it's sorta our fault. At Halloween, we always have a haunted forest to raise funds for animal shelters. Some of our costumes are really cool and realistic."

"And scary," Brittany added.

"But that's all pretend. I think Mason and his dad are serious about hunting werewolves," I insisted.

"So? They won't find anything. Meanwhile, we get paid," Lindsey said.

"I guess. It just makes me a little wary of them."

"People believe all kinds of things. As long as they aren't violent, who does it hurt? And rumors like this bring people to the park. It's all good."

I supposed she made sense. I adjusted the weight of my pack on my shoulders. I was proud of the fact that I was able to keep up with everyone. Rafe was the last one on the trail, making sure that no one got left behind.

"So, uh, Lucas. Does he do the whole haunted forest thing?" I asked. I couldn't imagine it. He seemed so serious that I couldn't imagine him playacting.

"He did before he went off to college," Lindsey said. "Now he just comes home for the holidays and summer. Are you interested in him?"

"What? No." I laughed self-consciously. "Just curious. We're all going to be spending the summer together. Seems like we should know things about each other."

"Maybe tonight around the campfire, we can play Truth or Dare," Brittany said.

"Hey, you're lagging behind," Connor yelled from the top of the trail, and we picked up our pace.

I was hoping that Brittany was teasing about Truth or Dare. There was a lot I wanted to know, but not a lot I wanted to share.

As it turned out, we didn't play any games around the campfire. Nor did Dr. Keane or Mason mention werewolves.

Later that night as Brittany and I were in the tent getting ready for bed, Lindsey slipped inside with an air of excitement. "Okay, guys, I got up close and personal with Ethan and I know what's in the crate. Beer."

"You're kidding," Brittany said. "That's it?"

"Well, there's equipment, too, but they're smuggling beer in the empty spaces and they've decided it's too heavy to haul, so as soon as Dr. Keane turns in for the night"—she gave a big grin—"party time!"

Brittany and I immediately stopped our preparations for bed and began preparing to go back outside with the guys. I hadn't planned on us having a party in the wilds, but I was excited about it. I brushed out my hair and left it loose to curl wildly around my shoulders. Then I began scrounging through my backpack for my emerald-green halter top.

Lindsey peered out the tent opening. "What is with Dr. Keane tonight? Go to bed already."

"You gonna hook up with Ethan again?" Brittany asked. Her shining black hair hung past her shoulders.

"No. And I didn't hook up with him earlier. I just flirted a little bit."

"For someone who is supposed to be committed to Connor, you don't seem to take it very seriously."

"What?" I asked, finally clutching the halter. "You and Connor? You never said anything." I'd seen them together a couple of times, but hadn't been sure it was romantic.

"It's complicated," Lindsey said, and I could hear the frustration in her voice. She finished brushing out her blond hair, then rolled up the ends of her shirt and tied them in a knot so her belly button showed. It seemed we all wanted to attract a little attention tonight. "My parents and his parents, they're old friends and so they're pushing us together."

"If you don't want to be pushed, push back," Brittany said.

"You'd like that, wouldn't you?"

"I just think he deserves someone who wants to be with him."

"And that would be you?"

"Whoa, girlfriends, are we about to have a catfight here?" I asked.

They glared at each other. Lindsey backed down first. Maybe because Brittany woke up early every morning and went through a rigorous strengthening routine.

"Connor and I aren't sure where we're going to take this. So can we be cool about it until this trip is over?"

Brittany shrugged. "Whatever."

Every now and then I'd sensed some tension between them. This explained a lot. I wondered if Brittany liked Connor.

I slipped on my green halter and some white shorts. In a way, I sympathized with Lindsey. Sometimes it was difficult to know exactly what you felt for someone. At that moment I wasn't certain if I was trying to make myself attractive for Lucas or Mason. I'd felt a connection with Lucas last night, but he still overwhelmed me. Mason . . . well, Mason just seemed less complicated.

I wished I had some sexy sandals to wear, but all I had were my hiking boots. They'd have to do. But looking in the small mirror that I had, I was pleased with the way everything looked.

Lindsey looked back outside. "Finally! Dr. Keane is gone. Let's go."

Everyone was creeping out of the camp like ninja warriors or something. Each of the grad students, including Monique, was carrying a six-pack of beer. Only the tiniest sliver of a moon was in the sky, so Connor led the way with a flashlight. When we got far enough from camp that Dr. Keane wouldn't hear us, Ethan started passing out the cans of beer.

To my utter shock, even Lucas was there to grab one. Of course, he then went to find a tree to lean against. Monique joined him. He gave her one of his rare smiles. Jealousy sparked through me but I turned away, not wanting to acknowledge it. We'd shared a special moment last night, but obviously for him it had meant nothing more than a big-brother figure watching out for someone he was responsible for.

Lindsey tapped her can against mine. "To good times."

"Why didn't you tell me about you and Connor?" Okay, I was a little bummed. I'd told her plenty about me since we'd met last summer, including my nightmares. And she was holding back on some critical stuff here.

"Like I said, I don't know where it's going. And who wants to be set up by their parents?"

"It seems like Brittany is really into Connor."

"I think she might be. She's dealing with some stuff she's not talking about. You see all the exercising and toning she does, like she wants to be supersherpa or something. And okay, yeah, she did—does—like Connor, but he agrees with our parents, that we're supposed to be together. We were always friends when we were growing up. I don't want to hurt him, but I just don't know if he's the one, so right now I don't want to deal with it." She sipped her beer.

"How does Connor feel?"

"Disappointed that I'm not returning the enthusiasm. Like I said, it's complicated."

"I'm here anytime you want to talk."

She looked over at me and grinned. "Thanks." She again tapped her can against mine. "Think I'm going to go mingle with some hot students."

As she walked away, as much as I hated to admit it, it was a little reassuring and comforting to know I wasn't the only one who was screwed up.

"What's up?"

Peering over at Mason, who had suddenly appeared, I smiled. "Not much." I lifted my can. "Crazy for you guys to be hauling beer."

"No kidding. Ethan and Tyler were losing their enthusiasm for the idea." He looked up. "You know what I love about camping? How vast the sky looks at night.

Want to go stargazing? I found a spot away from the trees where we could lie on the grass. . . ." He tipped his head to the side in a questioning gesture.

I glanced over to where Lucas was talking with Monique. I'd definitely misread last night. Maybe since he was the one in charge, he thought he needed to steer clear of any emotional attachments. Or maybe I was nothing more than someone to look after—the newbie, someone he wasn't quite sure had what it took to be a sherpa.

"Sure," I said. "Why not?"

Mason and I each grabbed another beer. By the time we reached the spot he was talking about, I had a pleasant buzz going. The grass was cool and slightly damp with dew as I lay down on it.

"There's the Big Dipper," Mason said, pointing upward.

I pointed as well. "And there's Cassiopeia."

Mason groaned. "You know the constellations."

"Well, duh, yeah. It was the first thing my dad taught me when he took me camping."

"I was hoping to impress you, but now I have a confession to make. The Big Dipper is the only constellation I'm ever able to pick out. I never can connect the stars to form anything else."

I had a feeling that wasn't a problem Lucas had, that

he'd be able to identify more than I could. Why was I even thinking about Lucas now?

I rolled slightly toward Mason. "Okay, Cassie might be hard, but if you can find the Big Dipper, you ought to be able to make out Draco the Dragon. His tail curves down between the dippers."

"Nope."

"Follow the line of my finger. Right there."

"Nope. Sorry. I've never been good at seeing patterns inside pictures."

I rolled away from him. "Not important. The best part is the shooting stars anyway."

"Somehow I always miss them, too."

I laughed. "Mason! That's insane. We'll just have to stay out here until you see one."

"That could take all night," he said quietly.

I rolled my head toward him. I could see that he was watching me. "It definitely will if you're not looking at the sky."

"But you're more interesting." He paused. "What made you want to be a sherpa?"

"I like being in the woods, and this way I'm paid for being in the woods. It's a win-win."

"Since you're from Dallas, you probably don't know these other guys very well."

Was he trying to set up an us-versus-them tone? It

seemed counterproductive to our goal of getting Mason and his group safely to the area they'd identified as where they wanted to camp. On the other hand, maybe he was having doubts about the park employees. Or maybe he was just looking for conversation.

"I met them last summer," I assured him. "Lindsey and I have been emailing and calling each other ever since. We've become friends. I think because we have so much in common."

"Like what?"

"Our love of the outdoors, mostly. Plus we're both going to be seniors this year. And no matter where you go to high school, it's always the same. Cliques. Teachers. Homework. Guys." I thought again about Lindsey's situation. We'd talked about guys in general terms, but she'd never mentioned what was going on with her and Connor. I had to admit, I was slightly hurt that she hadn't confided in me.

"So you met all the guides last summer?" Mason asked.

"Yeah."

"I guess we're lucky to have them around," he said. "I never really considered how dangerous it is to be in the woods. Considering what happened to your parents, aren't you scared?"

"No. As strange as it seems, I've always felt safe here.

As long as you stay alert, you'll be okay. And the sherpas are paid to be alert. Besides, I'd trust Lucas with my life." I surprised myself by saying that out loud.

"Really?"

"Oh yeah. He's always so aware of things."

"He seemed pretty aware of Monique back there."

Not until she parked herself in front of him, I thought unkindly.

"You like Lucas?" he asked, maybe in response to my silence.

"I don't dislike him."

"You like me?"

I had a feeling he was asking something more.

Before I could answer, the hairs on the back of my neck and my arms prickled. I shot up to a sitting position.

"What is it?" Mason asked.

"We're being watched."

He scoffed. "Oh. Probably Lucas. That guy—"

"No, not Lucas." I wasn't sure how I knew it wasn't him—or perhaps a better way to say it was that I would know if it *were* him. The way he watched me felt very different. It felt protective. This seemed . . . threatening.

"We should probably go." I got to my feet.

"Thought we were going to wait until I spotted a shooting star."

"We haven't even been watching the sky. And seriously.

I've got a bad feeling. We need to get back."

"It's just because we started talking about danger."

I started rubbing my arms. "That's not it. Come on, Mason. Lucas is going to push us again tomorrow. I need to get some sleep."

He reluctantly scrambled to his feet. "Okay."

I grabbed the beer cans and shoved them into his arms. "They might be lighter, but you guys are still going to have to carry them. We can't trash the forest."

"Guess bringing beer wasn't such a smart idea after all." I could see his grin. "Except it gave me some time alone with you."

As we headed back to camp I couldn't shake the feeling that there was something watching us, something dangerous. Then I saw it, lost in the shadows of the trees a little ways away. Only its shining gray eyes were visible. A wolf. It poked its head out only a fraction, but it was enough for me to see that it was black. Solid black.

It was watching us.

Lucas had said that wolves didn't attack humans, but I wasn't so sure.

"Hey, I saw a wolf like that the night I followed you to the birthday party," Mason said.

"Really?"

"Yeah, I nearly had a heart attack, right on the spot.

It just stepped out of the shadows as I was heading back to the cabin."

What I was feeling tonight was a lot like what I'd felt that night. Why would a wolf be following me?

"You think it's dangerous?" Mason asked.

Yes! my mind screamed.

"I don't know," I replied. I did know that I didn't trust this wolf. Something about it sent off a signal that it was looking for trouble. Either that or I'd had one beer too many.

SIX

It was late the next afternoon when we reached the roaring river. The water flowed rapidly, creating cresting, white-capped waves. Even though it wasn't terribly deep, it appeared incredibly dangerous.

I watched with my heart in my throat as Lucas waded across it. A knotted rope secured to a tree on the bank was tied around his waist. If he slipped, it would stop him from being carried downstream. Once he arrived at the other bank, he'd secure it to another tree, forming a line across the river the rest of us could hold on to. He was almost midstream and the water was crashing wildly around his hips, which meant it would be at my waist, maybe even higher.

The element of danger sent adrenaline and a measure of excitement pumping through me. This was going to be fun, not to mention challenging. I loved the water almost as much as I loved hiking. I was anticipating testing my skills against the raging river.

"Hey, Kayla, want to help us over here?" Brittany asked.

I glanced over. They'd inflated a yellow raft and were loading the supplies onto it. Mason and his group were loading another raft with the crate they were hauling, a crate that was a little lighter today.

I knelt beside our raft and began lashing things down.

"You and Mason seemed pretty tight last night," Lindsey said.

"Just stargazing." I didn't know why I suddenly felt self-conscious about spending time with him. "He's never seen a shooting star."

"Yeah, right," Brittany said. "Campers are always using that excuse to get time alone with a sherpa."

"No, seriously," I insisted.

Brittany laughed lightly. "It's not a problem. He's cute."

She was right about that.

"Lucas will probably leave one of us behind to keep an

eye on them," Lindsey said.

"Is that normal?" I asked. Lindsey had stayed with us last summer, but we'd only been in the park for about a week.

"Yeah, especially if they go far into the wilderness like this group is doing. The last thing the park wants is a reputation for campers getting into trouble."

"Who'll stay behind?"

"Don't know yet. Whoever draws the short straw, probably," Brittany said. "Since you like Mason, maybe it'll be you."

A victorious yell echoed around us. It came from Connor and Rafe, who'd been standing at the bank, serving as spotters. I guessed if Lucas had lost his balance or went under, one of them planned to dive in after him. Not sure what good that would have done. . . .

But it was all moot. He'd made it safely to the other side. I wasn't sure why I felt so proud of him, as though his victory was mine. He tied off the rope before stripping off his T-shirt and hanging it over a bush to dry. Even from this distance, I could appreciate the beauty of his bare torso. It was early June and he was already sporting a perfect tan. He didn't strike me as a tanning booth kind of guy. He loved the outdoors as much as I did, so that tan was all natural.

As he turned, I also noticed something on his left back

shoulder. A birthmark? A tattoo? It looked too perfect. It had to be ink. *Isn't that interesting?* I wondered what he thought was important enough that he wanted it to be a permanent part of his body. I also couldn't deny that I found the idea of tattoos sexy—when they were well done. His, even from this distance, was definitely sexy.

"We're done over here," Mason said.

I startled at his sudden announcement and his nearness—as though I'd been caught doing something I shouldn't have been doing. Thank goodness he wasn't a mind reader. He wouldn't have appreciated my thoughts about Lucas. But then, how much loyalty did I owe Mason? We'd only watched the stars together.

"Kayla, have you got a second?" he asked.

I looked at Lindsey and Brittany. They both shrugged.

"We're almost done," Lindsey hesitantly offered, as though she wasn't sure if I was looking for an excuse not to leave.

I got up from my crouch and followed Mason a short distance until we were away from the others. "What's up?" I asked.

"Haven't really had much time to talk with you today. Wish Lucas would set you free."

I smiled. "He's not my prison guard."

"Then maybe when we get to the other side of the river, you can tell him you want to walk with me. Or maybe I should tell him."

"I don't know if he's open to suggestions like that, but I'll talk to him."

"Great. You know the problem with camping for a month is that it totally destroys your dating life. I mean, what if I wanted to ask you out on a date? It's not like we could go to the movies."

I grinned, thinking I might know where this was going—and feeling incredibly flattered. "That's true."

"But a candlelit dinner—"

"A can of beans over candlelight?"

"Hey, it's not the food, it's the company, and I did bring a candle. So maybe tonight . . ."

He let the words trail off, forming a safe question. *If I was interested . . .*

Was I? I shifted my gaze toward the water. Lucas was on his way back. I couldn't see him being romantic. Although he had been sweet that first night when I'd needed to wander.

Sweet? Not exactly a word I'd ever thought to associate with Lucas. Why was it that no matter what I was doing, I was thinking about him? It was insane, especially when I had a guy practically asking me out on a date— here in the wilderness.

"Dinner by candlelight tonight. Absolutely."

"Cool. We'll sneak away."

My inner adventure girl was feeling wicked. "Great. I'll catch you later."

I walked back over to where Lindsey and Brittany were tucking a few more things into the raft. The thought was that the less we all had to carry, the easier it would be for us to get across. Our backpacks, boots, and anything that would weigh us down went into the raft.

Once three rafts were fully loaded, the guys hauled them into the water. Lucas, Connor, and Rafe struggled to get the supply raft across the river. Behind them, Dr. Keane, Mason, and Ethan waged their own battle against the river as they guided their raft of secret equipment. David, Jon, and Tyler were pushing the last raft, which carried the grad students' backpacks and miscellaneous items.

The rest of us waited on the bank of the river.

"Talk about sexist—like we're not strong enough to get the rafts across," Monique said.

"Works for me," Lindsey said. "Let them do all the hard work."

"Easy for you to say. You don't have to impress Dr. Keane. I can't wait until we reach our destination and can really get down to business."

"And what is that exactly?" I asked. I was still a little confused about what they planned to achieve.

"Discovering the source of the werewolf legend in this

wilderness. It's part of Dr. Keane's academic focus."

"You think you're going to find a book lying around somewhere?"

She gave me an indulgent smile. "Something like that. They know we're coming. The wolves. Don't you hear them at night?"

I thought about the one I'd seen last night. I wondered if I should mention it to Lucas. Something about the wolf seemed ominous. If it was rabid, it probably would have attacked. I was probably just getting more wary as we got farther away from civilization, out of my comfort zone.

"Wolves howl," Brittany said. "It's what they do."

"Whatever." Monique nodded toward the river. "Lucas is so hot. I can't believe he doesn't have a girlfriend."

"I think he's one of those guys who believes in waiting for the right girl," Lindsey said.

"Yeah, right. The strong, silent type? Always a player. Take it from me. I've seen enough of them on campus to know."

"You go to the same university?" I asked, surprised by her words.

"No, we're from Virginia. Lucas said he's going to school in Michigan."

"Yep," Lindsey said. "Track scholarship."

"Guess I could always transfer," Monique said, never

taking her eyes off him as he and the others hauled the rafts onto the bank.

"Okay, looks like it's our turn to head across," Brittany said.

Lindsey and I stepped into the river. The cold water was powerful as it streamed around my calves. Lindsey and I reached back to give Brittany and Monique a handhold and helped steady them against the rushing water. When they were on their way across, Lindsey saluted me and began to make her way toward the distant shore.

Lucas had designated that I go last. I didn't fool myself into thinking that he thought I was special. He'd probably read my sherpa application and knew I was a strong swimmer. I'd been on the high school swim team and had tried out for the Olympic team. I missed making it by a few hundredths of a second. So although no one was watching my back, I wasn't worried.

Since we were leaving Dr. Keane's group and would return to the ranger village using this route, we were just going to keep the rope secured here so it would be ready when we got back to this spot. Most of our supplies would remain with Dr. Keane, so we could move more swiftly heading back.

I waited until Lindsey was almost three fourths of the way across before I started making my way. I gripped the rope hard and fought against the powerful rushing water.

Without the rope, I knew I couldn't have kept my balance, couldn't have stayed upright. The currents were wild and turbulent. The water had risen to my waist when I felt a quick tug on the rope. The strange vibration reminded me of the way the fishing line grew taut when I went fishing with my adoptive dad and we had a nibble.

Brittany and Monique had made it to shore. Lindsey continued on—she hadn't felt the unusual jerk on the rope, as it had started behind me and traveled only up to my hand. Suddenly I felt another one of those strange sensations of being watched that had dogged me ever since that first night when Lindsey had arranged the surprise party for me. In spite of the warnings sounding inside my head, I stopped and glanced back. Because it was so late in the afternoon, the shadows were lengthening. I couldn't see anything. I supposed it could have been a bird—a big bird—landing and flying off.

"Kayla!"

Even over the roaring of the river, I recognized Lucas's voice and the impatience in it. I turned back toward the distant shore. Lindsey was just making her way out of the water. I knew why Lucas was upset with me. I was the holdup. Lucas wanted to make some more progress before nightfall. The guy didn't know the meaning of meandering or taking it easy. With him it was all about pushing to the limits, his limits and—

The rope suddenly snapped. The tumultuous water pushed my legs out from beneath me and I dropped beneath it. I lost my hold on the lax rope and started frantically searching for it. It was gone. But worst of all, I couldn't draw in air. I was completely submerged and caught in the current. My lungs were burning, my chest tightening.

I fought to get my footing, but the chaotic water was propelling me along. I couldn't find the river bottom. I must have gone into deeper—

Slam!

I hit a boulder or a rock or something incredibly huge and hard. It knocked the last of my breath out of me. I started battling to get to the surface. My lungs were on fire; my chest was aching. I didn't know if it was going to cave in or explode. It felt like it was capable of doing both at the same time.

I broke through to the surface, gasped for air, and went back under the water. I had to get control. I fought back the rising panic and the fear of dying.

I'm not going to drown. I refuse to drown.

I struggled to lift my face out of the roiling current and rolled to my back. Where had the turbulent rapids come from? The water moved faster here. It was stronger. How far had I traveled? It seemed like miles.

Out of the corner of my eye, I caught sight of a large branch floating nearby. I lunged for it. It kept me afloat, gave me a chance to gather my thoughts and my breath. I had to get to the bank. I kicked, trying to use the branch as a floatation device, but the rapids were playing with it as though they owned it. I let it go and began trying to swim to shore.

I wasn't that far away. I could do this. I could make it.

Something scraped along my knee. It stung, but it also made me realize the water was suddenly shallower. The current was still strong, pushing me along the rocky bottom, keeping my feet from gaining stability. I dragged myself until I was almost to shore. Then I lurched up and over the edge, onto the grassy bank.

My stomach and chest ached as I coughed up water. Then I collapsed, breathing heavily. I hurt all over. My arms and legs were scraped raw and bleeding in places. I began shivering, not only from the cold but from the shock of it all. I didn't want to think about how close I'd come to drowning. I'd taken water rescue classes a couple of summers ago when I'd worked as a lifeguard at the city pool, but the river was more dangerous than a pool. I'd been lucky . . . so far. I knew from the survival classes I'd taken that I didn't have the luxury of resting. It was imperative that I get warm.

I forced myself to sit up. I squeezed as much water as I could out of my clothes, but it brought no immediate relief.

I wanted to just lie down and sleep, but I knew I had to

begin making my way back to the others. Running would help heat my body. I needed heat. I struggled to my feet and staggered forward through the trees.

A loud ominous growl froze me in my steps.

I'd thought the river would be the most dangerous thing I'd face today. I'd been very, very wrong.

An angry bear was much worse.

SEVEN

The bear was huge! Standing on its hind legs, it looked like it was close to seven feet tall—although my perception of its height could have been skewed by my terror. I didn't know if bears reacted to the smell of blood or fear, but I was still bleeding—and I was definitely scared.

I'd read that if you were confronted by a bear the best approach was to drop to the belly and stretch out. Although I'd also read to curl into a fetal position. Decisions, decisions. I was still recovering from the ordeal in the river and could barely think, let alone decide which strategy to follow. I did know enough not to panic or run. But I couldn't bring myself to go submissive. If anything happened, I wanted to be in a position to at least try to save my life.

Shaking its head, the bear opened its mouth and roared. Its teeth were huge and its paws were monstrous. Then it dropped to all fours and began to charge.

Instinctively, I turned to run. Out of the corner of my eye, I caught a blur of movement. A low threatening growl—different from the bear's—reverberated through the area. I spun back around in time to see a wolf leap onto the bear.

Scrambling back, I tripped over something and landed hard on my butt. I thought I should use the distraction of the wolf's attack to run, but somehow I couldn't tear my gaze from the animals that were snarling and snapping at each other. The bear slapped at the wolf. I heard it yelp and I could see streamers of blood on its hindquarters where the bear's claws had ripped through.

But it didn't back down as it crouched, placing itself between the bear and me. I didn't want this wolf to die. It wasn't the one I'd seen last night. Of that I was certain. Its fur was different, a mixture of colors. It bared its teeth.

Standing on its hind legs, the bear growled. The wolf snapped, a low warning sound vibrating from its throat.

I knew I should have been running, but I just didn't have the energy. Now that I was back on the ground, I didn't know if I'd ever be able to get up. I wanted to scream. I wanted one of the sherpas to find me, to help me.

The bear made another swipe at the wolf, tossing it in the air as though it were nothing. After landing hard, the wolf scrambled up, went into a crouch, and began circling the bear. Then it sprung forward, went in low, and nipped the bear on the leg. The bear released a little yelp, turned tail, and ran.

Still crouching, the wolf turned toward me. Was I about to become its victim? I remembered what Lucas had said: A healthy wolf had never attacked a human. I tried not to cower. I didn't want it to sense that I had reservations, that I was wary of it. But exhaustion, fear, and everything I'd endured since the rope snapped were claiming me, and I began trembling violently.

Trying to regain control of myself, I focused on the wolf rather than on how badly I hurt. It reminded me of a big dog. It was the most beautiful creature I'd ever seen. Its fur was a strange mixture of deep, luminous colors. And its eyes were a lively silver, not the dull gray of the wolf I'd seen last night. I had this odd sensation that it was looking me over, trying to determine—what? Why was it watching me? Why was it just standing there?

The longer it stood there, the more comfortable I became with it. I felt this strange sort of bonding that I couldn't exactly explain. The wolves in my nightmares were always fierce, but this one had saved me, had put itself between me and the bear. All these years had I let what happened to my parents affect my dreams? I was afraid of something, but it wasn't the wilderness or this wolf. It was something inside me, something I didn't understand.

I heard a cacophony of voices. The others. I thought of Dr. Keane and his obsession with wolves.

"Run," I whispered harshly. "Be safe."

He turned his head at a quizzical angle. Then he bolted away, disappearing behind the dense foliage.

"Kayla!" Lindsey yelled.

"Here!" I stayed where I was, striving to gather my strength.

"Oh my God!" Lindsey cried as she, Brittany, Rafe, Connor, and Mason broke into the clearing. I was surprised Lucas wasn't in the group.

Lindsey rushed over to me, dropped to her knees, and began rubbing my arm, careful to avoid the scrapes. It felt so good.

"We were afraid you'd drowned," Brittany said as she joined Lindsey and began rubbing my other arm. The additional warmth was heavenly.

I gave a weak laugh. "No."

Rafe removed his shirt. "You should take off your wet shirt."

Lindsey snatched his shirt and shooed the guys away. "Lucas has ink like that," I heard Mason say as they walked away.

On the left shoulder of Rafe's back was a tattoo,

something that looked like a Celtic symbol. Very much like the necklace I wore. I touched it now, relieved to find that I hadn't lost it in the river.

"Yeah, frat initiation," Rafe said. "Crazy, huh?"

Considering the circumstances, my first thought was wildly insane: I couldn't picture Lucas joining a fraternity. The thought after that was that he'd stayed behind with the others and the supplies, rather than make sure I was okay. I couldn't squash my disappointment.

Lindsey nudged my shoulder, bringing me back from my distracted musings. "Come on. We need to get you out of these wet clothes."

I took off my shirt and bra. Brittany bundled them up while I drew on Rafe's shirt. It still carried his body heat and was as comforting as a warm blanket. It made me feel so much better. My shorts were made of a quick-drying material, and while I wasn't toasty, I wasn't nearly as chilled as I had been.

Once I was wearing Rafe's shirt, the guys came back over.

"Should we build a fire here or just get her back to camp?" Connor asked.

"Get her back to camp," Rafe said. "Can you carry her?"

"Yeah, sure," Connor responded.

"I can walk," I insisted. "The movement will help warm me up some more, don't you think?"

"Yeah, probably," Connor said. "Can you stand? Start moving around?"

I nodded and he pulled me to my feet.

"What about Lucas?" Mason asked. "The way he was running shouldn't he have beat us here?"

He isn't at the camp? He came after me?

I felt this small spark of joy that made my eyes sting. How weird was that? Another delayed reaction to the trauma. That's what it had to be. I wasn't special to Lucas; he wasn't special to me, except in a we-are-sherpas kind of bond.

"He probably lost sight of Kayla in the water and ran right past where she ended up coming to shore," Rafe explained. "The guy's going to university on a track scholarship. He runs like the wind. I'll search down a little farther, see if I can find him. You guys head back. Kayla needs to drink something warm—the sooner, the better."

He didn't wait for anyone to argue with him. He just started walking in the direction that the wolf had gone.

"Be careful!" I called out. "There was a wolf and a bear."

Rafe stopped as though he wanted to say something, but Mason beat him to it. "Where?"

"Here. They fought. They both ran off. The wolf is hurt. If you run across him—"

"Don't worry. I won't approach him. Wild animals and I don't get along." He hurried away to try to find Lucas to let him know I was okay.

When we got back to camp, I was glad to see that the tents were set up. I slipped into mine. I couldn't get out of my damp shorts fast enough. I pulled on some warm flannel pants and a sweatshirt. The scratches I'd received were no longer bleeding, but I put some antiseptic on them. Couldn't be too careful in the woods. Then I grabbed a blanket, wrapped it around me, and went out to sit by the fire. I needed some comfort food. A big bag of Double Stuf Oreos would be nice. But alas, I hadn't packed our provisions.

Lindsey handed me a mug of soup. "Drink that. It'll help warm you."

She sat beside me. "We were so worried."

"Not as worried as I was."

"Okay, don't take this wrong, but I'm glad it was you and not me. I'm not a strong swimmer."

"If swimming the rapids is ever an Olympic event, I might have another chance to make the team."

She laughed, getting my corny joke, because I'd shared with her my almost making the Olympic team. "Most definitely."

She put her arm around me and hugged me tightly. "God, I don't know if I've ever been so scared for someone in my entire life."

I laid my head on her shoulder. I thought I could go to sleep right there. The only thing that I would have found more comforting was Lucas's shoulder. I was touched that he'd been in such a panic to find me that he'd raced right past me. He'd probably be angry with himself when he realized what had happened. He wasn't perfect. Not that I planned to point that out to him.

Lucas and Rafe strolled into camp with an easy stride. With their dark coloring, they looked almost like brothers.

"I was right," Rafe said, "he'd run faster than the river had carried you downstream. He went right past the area where you came ashore."

"That's what you get for holding the university record in the mile," Connor said.

Lucas barely acknowledged Connor's remark before crouching beside me. "You okay?"

"Yeah," I answered, embarrassed by all the attention. "I didn't mean to cause so much fuss. I don't know why the rope gave way."

"They didn't tell you?"

I gave him a confused look. "Tell me what?"

"The rope was cut."

EIGHT

"What are you talking about?" Dr. Keane demanded.

For a minute, looking into Lucas's eyes, I'd almost forgotten that we weren't alone.

"After Lucas took off, Connor and I pulled the rope to shore," Rafe said. "We thought maybe the rope had rubbed against the bark and become frayed, but the edges were even. Someone used a knife on it."

"Who'd do such a thing?" Monique asked.

Lucas unfolded his body in that predatory way he had. "Do you have any enemies, Professor?"

"One of my colleagues and I compete for grants, but I hardly think he's the type to sabotage our expedition,"

Dr. Keane said calmly, but his gaze was darting around the sherpas as though he were looking for something suspicious. "It doesn't make sense for *anyone* to feel threatened by what we're doing. I suggest we all turn in. We lost some time today as a result of this little . . . mishap. I'd like to make it up tomorrow."

I'd almost died and he considered it an inconvenient *mishap*? And he wanted to ignore all the implications of a cut rope? Even if I wasn't sure what it all meant, I thought it might bear talking about.

Mason gave me a look that said he wanted to say something. Maybe he wanted to apologize for his father.

With groans and grumblings, the students headed into their tents. All except Mason. I could tell that whatever he wanted to say to me, he didn't want to say it with an audience. I took pity on him. It wasn't his fault his dad was a jerk.

I pushed myself to my feet and walked over to him. I forced a tired smile. "I guess the candlelit dinner isn't going to happen."

His cheeks turned a dark hue as he blushed. "Not tonight, but maybe we could take a short walk?"

I nodded and we started strolling away from the fire.

"Don't go beyond sight of the camp," Lucas ordered gruffly.

I glanced over my shoulder at him. He didn't look happy. I had almost died and everyone's mood had soured.

I didn't know whether to be flattered that I had so much influence or irritated. "We won't."

"He sure is protective of you," Mason said as we headed just beyond the camp.

"He's protective of everyone. It's his job."

"You should have seen him streaking off when you were washed away. I've never seen anyone move like that, almost a blur."

"Apparently he's some badass track star."

"Yeah, apparently so." We stopped when we were far enough away that no one would hear us. He took my hand, the one that wasn't clutching the blanket. "I was going to race off with him, but Rafe held me back. There was no way I could have kept up with him anyway."

"That's okay. You were there when I needed you to be."

"I tried, but all the sherpas are so protective of you that they make me feel like an outsider."

"It's okay, really." I hated that he felt so badly about all that—and that he'd wanted to be there for me, but the others hadn't let him. I knew he didn't feel completely comfortable around them. I figured it was because he was such an academic. He was pretty young to be in grad school already. He probably had an amazingly high IQ.

"So what came first—the wolf or the bear?" he asked.

"Is this a chicken-or-the-egg question?" I didn't bother

to keep the irritation out of my voice. It seemed like such an odd question.

"Seriously. I'm just curious. I mean, bears don't usually attack."

"Tell that to the Boy Scout who was attacked in Alaska a few years back." I suddenly realized that my irritation with him was as stupid as his question. What did any of it matter? I was alive. "The bear."

"So there was a bear, and then a wolf came to your rescue?"

"I don't know that he came to my rescue. I mean, yeah, he chased off the bear, but maybe he just didn't like bears." I tried to laugh it off. "Might have nothing to do with me. I'm not even sure he knew I was there until afterward."

"What did the wolf look like?"

This was getting so ridiculous. I tugged my hand free. "It was black."

"Just black? Like the one we saw last night?"

No, I thought. But I didn't want to tell him that. I didn't know why. I felt protective of the wolf I'd just seen. "What were you expecting?"

He shifted his gaze to where the sherpas were still waiting around the campfire. Dr. Keane didn't tell *us* when to go to bed. I had a feeling that tonight, just to be obstinate, they'd stay up really late—and probably not be quiet about it.

"I don't know," he said quietly, "I thought maybe it would be a mixture of colors." He leaned toward me and lowered his voice even more. "Between you and me, I find it odd that *Lucas* didn't find you before we got there." *What was he talking about?*

I remembered the conversation he'd had with his father that first night. Was he thinking Lucas . . . was the *wolf*? That was just insane!

Was this conversation really happening? Obviously, I'd suffered some oxygen deprivation while I'd been under the water.

"I think if Lucas was running fast and I was under water—which I was for a while—he could have lost sight of me."

"Maybe," Mason muttered. "There's just something odd about this whole thing."

"Whatever. I'm tired."

"I'm sorry. I didn't really bring you over here to give you the third degree. I was just curious. A lot of unexplained things happen in this forest."

"People play tricks on campers all the time, trying to freak them out. Like telling ghost stories around the campfire."

"I guess." He smiled at me. "I'm glad you're okay. I was actually a little jealous thinking of Lucas coming to your rescue. I'm really glad he pulled that idiot move and went too far. Means he's not perfect."

I touched his arm. "No need to be jealous."

"Maybe we'll have that date tomorrow night."

"Maybe."

He leaned forward like he was going to kiss me. Then stopped. Probably because he felt the same thing I did. Without even turning around, I knew Lucas was watching.

I saw the determination light up Mason's eyes, and I knew he was going to kiss me. He wanted to do it to get even with Lucas for something. But I wasn't playing that game. Before he could turn his attention back to me, I said, "Goodnight"—and walked away.

This camp is on testosterone overload.

I was almost to my tent when Lucas said, "Hey, Kayla, can you join us for a sec?"

The words formed a question; his tone didn't. It was a command. I was physically and mentally exhausted. Still, I shored up my reserves and trudged over to where he and the other sherpas were gathered. I wondered what was up with their secretive expressions. I had the feeling that whatever they'd been discussing, they didn't want the Keane group to know.

"How are you doing?" Lucas asked. True concern was reflected in his voice. I blinked back the tears that wanted to reveal my weakness. I was still trying to prove myself, not only to Lucas but also to the other guides. Lindsey gave me a reassuring smile.

"I'm doing okay. I owe that wolf my life. You heard about that, right? With the bear?"

"Yeah, Rafe told me. Sorry I wasn't around to be more help."

"You never struck me as someone who would panic and keep running without looking back." Even as I said the words, realizing I probably shouldn't have said them with the other sherpas standing around listening, I knew they were true. Lucas didn't panic. Ever. He didn't make stupid mistakes.

"The water was going so fast that I thought you were farther down. I didn't think to slow down and make sure."

I nodded, even though the words didn't ring true.

"I'd leave the wolf a steak if I could," I said.

"I'm sure he'd appreciate it. Anyway, I called you over because we wanted to know if you saw anything—noticed anything strange on the riverbank before you started to cross over."

Glancing around at the serious faces of the sherpas, I shook my head. "I had a second to glance back before I went under, but it was just shadows. Why would someone try to sabotage this expedition? It doesn't make any sense."

"We're not sure it's the expedition," Rafe said. "We're

thinking it might be someone with a grudge against the sherpas, against us."

"That's not exactly true," Lucas said. "It's a grudge against me."

"Why would someone have a grudge against you?" I asked. "I mean, you're Mr. Congeniality."

His teeth flashed white as he smiled. "Cute."

Yeah, I thought, *you absolutely are when you grin like that.*

"So—seriously. Who would hold a grudge?" I asked.

"Devlin. He was a sherpa here last summer. He did some stuff he shouldn't have done, took chances, put campers at risk," Brittany explained.

"Lucas kicked his butt," Connor said. He sounded so in awe that I was surprised he didn't give Lucas a fist bump.

"After which, Devlin took a hike." Apparently Rafe wanted to add to the story.

"But that doesn't mean he hasn't returned or that he's not hanging around," Lindsey warned.

Reflexively, everyone glanced around. It seemed strange that they were concerned about some slacker sherpa from last summer. Why would he be here now? *I* was the newbie. *I* was supposed to be nervous. *They* weren't. It gave me a bad feeling about everything.

"We'd know if he were around," Connor said.

"Not if he stayed far enough back," Lindsey responded.

"Lindsey has a point," Lucas said.

"Not to add to the paranoia that's being stirred up here, but I keep getting a sense that I'm being watched," I told them.

"That's right," Lindsey murmured. "That first night, she was all spooked—"

"I wasn't spooked. It just felt like someone was watching. And last night, too."

"What about last night?" Lucas asked.

"When we were drinking the beer, I had a sense that someone was watching. I mean, I saw a wolf later—"

"What color?"

"Mason just asked me the same question about the wolf that attacked the bear. Is there something going on with the wolves in the park that I need to know about? You said they don't attack people."

"They don't, but we've had some reports of at least one that warrants watching. So what color was the wolf you saw?"

"Last night it was hard to tell. If I had to guess I'd say black, but it could have been just the night shadows. The thing is, Mason was with me last night when I saw the wolf. He said he saw the same wolf—or at least he thinks it was the same wolf—hanging around the night of my birthday party."

"Mason was out in the woods during the party?" Lindsey asked. "And the wolf?"

"Mason said he couldn't sleep. But I don't think he's what I felt watching me. I think it was the wolf, because I had that same creepy feeling last night." I gave a small laugh. "Of course, a wolf couldn't cut a rope, so I don't know that all this means anything."

Lucas exchanged a strange look with Rafe.

"What?" I asked.

"Devlin had a pet wolf," Lucas said. "If it's around, there's a good chance that Devlin is, too. Everyone needs to stay alert. We'll start posting guards at night. Rafe and Brittany, you're up first."

A few minutes later, it felt great to crawl into my sleeping bag. I was battered and bruised, but remarkably I hadn't suffered any major cuts or scrapes. All in all, I'd been incredibly fortunate.

With that realization, my thoughts shifted to the wolf. I wondered if he was off somewhere nursing his wounds. Was there a female wolf waiting for him somewhere? Didn't wolves mate for life? Were they more loyal than humans?

"Kayla?" Lindsey whispered.

I rolled over without thought, groaning as my muscles and bruised skin protested. Last summer we'd shared a tent and talked late into the night. As much as I liked Brittany, I wasn't as close to her as I was to Lindsey, and I had a feeling Lindsey wasn't quite comfortable talking about everything with Brittany in the tent. "Yeah?"

"What do you think of Rafe?"

Of all the things I'd expected her to ask, after everything that had happened today, that question hadn't even popped up on my radar. "I think he's nice. Why?"

"I don't know. He's been around forever. I've grown up with him. It's just that he seems—different. More in command than usual. I mean, I've been thinking about him a lot—and it's just weird."

"You mean you like him?"

"Yeah, I think so."

"What about Connor?"

"I know. I don't want to hurt him. I really don't, but I just don't know if he's the right one for me."

"Do you have to decide this summer?"

"It's sort of a tradition in our families that you figure out by the time you're seventeen who you're supposed to be with. My birthday's coming up."

"That is so . . . medieval."

She released a tight laugh. "Yeah, I know. I just wish Lucas had paired me—instead of Brittany—up with Rafe as guards tonight. It's not any fun at all to be paired up with Connor. We haven't been getting along lately."

I furrowed my brow. "Maybe he'll pair me up with Connor to guard later on."

"Yeah, right. Do you not see the way Lucas looks at you? You are definitely sharing guard duty with him."

Suddenly the inside of my sleeping bag was way too warm. I slipped my leg out and rolled onto my side, half in and half out of my bag. "I don't know that it means anything. I mean, sometimes I get the impression that he considers me a lot of trouble. Besides, he's pretty hot. He probably has a girlfriend."

"I've never seen him with anyone more than a couple of times. He's never gotten serious with a girl. At least, not that I know of."

"I'm not even sure he likes me. Seriously. He's always barking at me."

She laughed lightly. "Literally?"

"What? No. He's just moody, but then I guess he has a lot of responsibility."

"Not only that, I'm sure he's trying to live up to everyone's expectations. His family is pretty powerful in the area."

"I didn't know that."

"Oh yeah. The Wildes pretty much rule things."

"Have they lived around here long?"

"For sure. Old family. They've been here, like, since the Civil War or something."

"I wonder if they were around when my parents were killed. My therapist says I need to face my past, but it's a little hard when I don't have clear memories of it and I don't know anyone who was there."

"That must have been hard. Watching your parents die. I can't even imagine . . ."

"I didn't actually see them die. Mom had shoved me back into this"—an image came to me and with it came sounds, smells—"into this little cave or something. There was growling." *Were* there wolves? Had the hunters shot at them and hit my parents? Was my mother trying to protect me?

"Do you know exactly where it happened in the park?"

I shook my head. "No. I didn't ask anyone last year. I don't think I really wanted to face the specifics. It was enough just to come here. But this year . . . I can't explain it, Lindsey, but I feel different. I feel like I'm *supposed* to be here. That I'm on the verge of some discovery."

"Like what?"

"I'm not sure. But that wolf today . . . I wasn't afraid of him. It was like I knew him. How weird is that?"

"Were wolves there when your parents were killed?"

"I didn't think so. I thought the hunters were just crazy. But I've been having these snippets of memory and there are wolves, but they aren't rabid or anything."

"Maybe you need to relax with those thoughts. Let them take you wherever."

"Maybe." I released a deep breath. "I'm too tired to think about it clearly tonight. I feel like I'm about to crash from the adrenaline rush."

She reached out and squeezed my hand. "I'm just glad you're okay."

"Me, too." I smiled at her. "Night."

I rolled back over and tried to go to sleep, but I was thinking about the wolf again. Why had he seemed so familiar? Had my real parents and I discovered a den of wolves? Maybe some cubs? Were my parents trying to protect them from the hunters? I wished I could remember more about that day. How long did wolves live? Why did I feel a connection with this one?

Then I heard a lonesome howl, and I somehow knew, *knew*, it was *him* calling to me. I felt this stirring deep down in my chest. I wanted to sit up, throw my head back, and howl in return. I wanted to answer his call. My strange reaction to his howl was frightening. It was as though he was calling out to some primal part of me that I hadn't even realized existed.

Face your fears, Dr. Brandon had said.

It was difficult to do when they constantly changed. Originally, they all centered around my past and what had happened with my parents. These fears brought forth the nightmares. But lately my fears had more to do with my future, with the unknown, with this strange stirring deep inside me. Sometimes I just felt as though I was going through changes that I couldn't understand. And I didn't know who to talk with about them, because I couldn't pinpoint exactly what was happening.

But I did know one thing: I wasn't afraid of that wolf. I slipped out of my bedroll and pulled on my boots. Lindsey didn't stir. I grabbed my first aid kit and flashlight before creeping outside. Brittany and Rafe were standing on the far side of the camp talking, not really paying attention. And even if they did spot me, they were watching for any danger that might come into the camp. I certainly wasn't a threat to anyone, and we weren't forbidden from leaving.

I hesitated a moment and thought about going to get Lucas, but I didn't plan to walk far. I didn't think I'd need to. I scurried around to the side of the tent and then strode out into the thicket, using the flashlight to guide me until I reached a spot far enough from camp that my talking voice wouldn't be heard, but close enough that my scream would be. I switched off my flashlight and waited. It was silly to think, to hope, that the wolf would come.

A crescent moon shone down on me. It was enough to see by. In the city, I had never realized how bright moon-light could be—or maybe it was just that my eyes were getting better at adjusting to the darkness—but my night vision was somehow keener.

Suddenly I heard a gentle padding. It seemed my ears were more alert as well. I shifted my eyes to the side, and there he was.

I dropped down to one knee, wishing I'd brought him something to eat. The moonlight gleamed along his multicolored fur as though drawn into it. "Hey, fella."

My voice caught with an edge of self-consciousness. I talked to Fargo, my Lhasa at home, all the time. But this was different. This was an animal of the wild, yet he didn't seem threatening. I didn't want to make any sudden moves, didn't want to frighten him. "I wanted to thank you."

To my amazement, he eased a little closer, close enough that I could pet him. I hesitated, before slowly burying my hand into his thick pelt. On top the fur was stiff, but underneath it was soft and comforting. Working to keep my voice calm and even, I said, "Don't be afraid. I know you got hurt. I want to see how bad it is."

I wasn't exactly sure what I could do to help. Try to clean it, put a little antiseptic on it? I was afraid if I bandaged it, he would be more visible to predators. I knew wolves varied in color so they could hide in their surroundings more easily. I cooed softly as I moved down to his hindquarter—the one that had gotten hurt. I'd never been this close to a wild creature. It was thrilling and unnerving. I knew if he decided to attack me that I wouldn't stand a chance of surviving, but I also instinctually knew that he wouldn't hurt me. I didn't know an animal could be so still. I brushed my hand through his fur, expecting to feel matted fur and dried blood. But it felt the same as the fur at his shoulder. I reached for my flashlight and shone it on his backside.

There was no blood. Not a trace. That didn't make sense. I could have sworn he'd gotten hurt. I thought maybe if he'd gone into a river or pond, the blood might have washed away, but there should have been gouged flesh where the bear had clawed him. Very gently I moved his fur aside, but I could find no wound. Mystified, I sat back on my heels. "I guess it was the bear's blood."

It wasn't as though I'd fully recovered from the ordeal in the river—I could have been mistaken about what had really happened.

I looked at the wolf. His head was twisted around as he watched me. I said, "You're so beautiful. I'm glad you're all right, but you can't hang around here. You might get hurt." Especially if Dr. Keane or Mason spotted him. "You need to go back to your pack."

Suddenly he snapped his head forward. He gave a throaty growl.

"What is it, boy?" Then I chastised myself. Did I really

think he could understand what I was asking? That he could answer me?

He glanced back at me, before taking off like a speeding bullet. I'd been worried that maybe I'd just been unable to find the wound, but now I knew for certain that he wasn't hurt at all.

I sat there for a while, staring into the darkness where he'd disappeared. I'd seen TV specials about people who communed with wild animals, but this was my first experience. Part of me thought it should have felt weird, but at the same time, it had seemed almost natural—as though the wolf and I were somehow connected.

It was strange. Ever since I'd returned to the forest, I'd had this odd sense of belonging. I felt a protectiveness toward the wolves especially. It was more than the fact that they were beautiful. It was as though they had human qualities: They were intelligent, monogamous, family-oriented. Maybe it was that sense of family that drew me to the wolf. Having lost my parents, family was so important to me.

"Kayla?"

Startled by Lucas's unexpected voice, I twisted around. "Hey."

"What are you doing out here?"

My encounter with the wolf felt very personal and private. I didn't want to share it. Besides, I thought it was possible that he'd think I was a little psycho.

"Just another night of not being able to sleep." I pushed myself to my feet.

"I've been there—when you're so exhausted, you think you'll crash and instead you stay awake."

"It's a little irritating." Although I thought if I went back to my sleeping bag, I would crash. If he noticed the first aid kit, he didn't say anything. For all I knew, he'd seen me with the wolf and was just being nice, pretending to believe my lies.

"Do you ever sleep?" I asked.

"Not much. A bad habit I got into this year at college—spending way too much time studying, when I wasn't partying."

"Don't take this wrong, but I can't see you partying."

"My first semester away from home, I went a little wild. We all did. Me, Connor, and Rafe. On campus, they called us the wildmen. But by the end of the year, we'd settled down." He glanced around. "You mentioned seeing a black wolf last night. How about the wolf this afternoon? Was it black?"

"No." While I'd hesitated to tell Mason the wolf's true color, I knew that Lucas was all about protecting the wildlife. "His fur was different colors—kinda like your hair, actually. Black, brown, white."

"Most wolves have varying shades of fur, which is

the reason that the black wolf stands out. Probably not a good idea to go out alone until we spot that wolf and know he's not going to cause any harm."

"You say that as though you know the wolves."

"Over the years, we've seen a lot of them. Don't think we know them all, but some are friendlier than others."

I nodded. The wolf I'd begun to think of as mine certainly seemed as though he'd never harm me.

"I think the day's catching up with me," I said.

Without saying a word, Lucas walked me back to my tent. He waited while I crawled back inside.

I was right. It didn't take me long to go to sleep. I dreamed about the candlelit dinner that Mason had promised me. Only in my dream, it wasn't Mason sharing the dinner with me. It was Lucas.

NINE

Lindsey was right. My night watch shift was with Lucas.

"If you're not feeling up to it, I can keep watch alone," he said when I joined him in the middle of the camp after Lindsey had nudged me awake when she finished her shift.

"No, I'm fine."

He gave me a pointed look.

"Okay, so I'm not *fine*, but I'm capable of keeping watch without straining myself."

He gave me that little twitch of his lips that resembled a smile. "You need a jolt of caffeine before we get started? I've got some coffee going over here."

"Oh, that'd be great."

We sat on a log by the fire and he handed me a mug of coffee. It was a cool night, and the warmth of the fire felt wonderful. Lucas was leaning forward, his elbows on his thighs, both hands around his mug, his eyes on his coffee. His profile was to me. He was ruggedly handsome.

"I scare you, don't I?" he asked quietly.

If I'd already taken a sip of coffee, I'd have either spewed it or choked on it.

"You're kind of intense," I admitted.

He released a dark chuckle. "Yeah. I take protecting this stretch of wilderness seriously, and when people like the professor and his group come into it, I'm not sure they respect it like they should." He glanced over his shoulder at me. "I grew up here. I love it. Don't you feel the same about Dallas?"

"I've never really felt like I belonged," I confessed. "I've always felt more at home in the woods."

"So we have that in common."

It was strange to think we might have a bond. "So what are you majoring in?"

"Political science."

I arched a brow. "What? You're going to go into politics?"

He gave me a wry grin. "Trying to improve my communication skills."

I had to admit that he wasn't one for small talk, but once he started talking, I didn't think he had any problems communicating. As a matter of fact, I found myself enthralled whenever we got into a conversation. It was obvious that when he cared about something, he cared deeply.

"Lindsey said your dad was someone important in the community."

"Yeah, he's served as mayor of Tarrant and was on the school board, so I guess my interest in politics comes naturally. He's always had high expectations."

"Did he find out about you beating up that Devlin guy?"

"Yeah. He wasn't happy about it." He shook his head. "Parents. Sometimes, no matter what you do, you can't please them."

"Tell me about it."

We sat in silence for a minute, each of us sipping our coffee.

"The color of your hair reminds me of a fox I once saw," he said quietly.

"Thanks. I think. That was a compliment, right?"

He chuckled. "Yeah. Most definitely."

"I've never seen a fox in the wild."

"Maybe I'll show you one before summer is over."

"That would be nice." I really did think it would be.

Better than a candlelit dinner where the main entrée was a can of beans. Even as I pictured that, I felt guilty at making light of Mason's attempt to romance me. The funny thing was, given the choice between trudging through the woods searching for a fox and a candlelit dinner in the finest restaurant—I would choose the fox. I should have thought, "Lucas gets me. He's the one." Instead, I swallowed hard and decided to change the subject, because I had a feeling that when it came to relationships, Lucas wouldn't fool around. He would be as intense in love as he was with all things. I was still carrying around too much baggage to be intense with anyone. Maybe when I'd had a chance to unload some of it. . . .

"So you really think it was that Devlin guy who cut the rope?" I asked.

If my change in conversational topic surprised him, he didn't show it.

"It's the only thing that makes sense," he said.

"But see, it doesn't make *any* sense at all to me. Okay, so he got fired. Move on already."

"He's not going to move on, not until he gets even. Since I've been off at school, he's had to wait. This place, these woods—this is where he'll want to take his revenge."

"Revenge? Just because you kicked his butt? That seems a little extreme."

He released a harsh laugh. "Extreme? That's Devlin.

In some ways, I think he's borderline psychotic."

"But what did he accomplish by cutting the rope except spooking everyone?"

"For him, that's enough motive. Create chaos."

"Do you think Dr. Keane and his students will be safe when we leave them?"

"Yeah. Devlin wants to discredit me. He won't hurt them."

"You sound like you know him pretty well."

He turned his silver gaze back on me. "I should. He's my brother."

I felt like I'd taken a punch to the chest. My shock must have shown on my face, because he got up, tossed his coffee into the fire, and strode away. I thought he was going to disappear into the forest, but he stopped at the spot where I'd seen Rafe and Brittany serving as sentries.

So he'd fought with his brother and gotten him fired—turned him in for improper behavior. I set my mug aside, got up, and walked over to him. I touched his arm. "That must have been hard, not to look the other way."

He gave his head a quick shake. "It was like he morphed into Anakin Skywalker and went to the dark side or something. He was doing all kinds of crazy shit. He knows these woods as well as I do. He could hide out in them, survive in them, without anyone knowing he's here."

"His bad behavior isn't your responsibility." I sounded like Dr. Phil.

"I confronted him. Humiliated him." He touched my cheek. His fingers were warm against my skin. His eyes had darkened to the shade of pewter. "I really want to show you that fox, but my job right now is to get the professor to his destination, then I have to find Devlin and deal with him. I have to focus on that." He dropped his hand to his side. He looked uncomfortable, as though he had a lot more that he wanted to say, things it might be too soon to say.

"You should probably take up your sentry post over there," he said, indicating the opposite corner of the camp.

"Yeah, sure. Good idea."

Disappointment at his dismissal hit me hard. As I strode across the camp, I decided that whatever I felt for Lucas was just a passing thing. I had Mason's attention. I'd always been a one-guy girl.

Mason was it. Mason was safe. Lucas had demons to fight. Maybe when he'd reconciled things with his brother, he'd have time for me.

Or maybe this strange pull I felt for him would snap, like the rope over the river. Maybe it could be severed as neatly.

Yeah, right, Kayla Madison. Dr. Brandon was wrong.

You don't need to face your fears. You need to face reality.

Ever since your parents died, you've shut down all your feelings. Lucas scares you because with him, you feel again.

And when you feel, you can be hurt.

I never wanted to be hurt again. Mason wouldn't hurt me.

TEN

The next day, because I was still bruised and sore, we traveled at a slow, casual pace. I could sense the tension in all the sherpas. We'd decided not to mention our suspicions about Devlin to Dr. Keane and his group. That we suspected the rope was cut was all they needed to know. Lucas was convinced that once we left our group, they would be safe.

When we took our first break, I gingerly removed my backpack, set it on the ground, and sat on it. Joining me, Mason extended a handful of wildflowers. They weren't abundant in this area, so he'd had to leave the trail every now and then whenever he spotted one.

"Thought these might make you feel better," he said.

I took them from him and smelled them. "Thanks."

"They're different kinds."

"I can see that."

"Some of them weren't easy to spot, but I was keeping an eye out."

"That was sweet."

"It's against park policy to pick wildflowers," Lucas suddenly said.

As usual, I hadn't heard him approach, but he was standing over us.

"So fine me," Mason said. "It's not like there's a florist out here that I can call."

"There's only a few," I said. "I don't think he did any real harm."

Lucas narrowed his eyes at us. Without another word, he walked away.

"What a romantic guy," Mason mumbled.

Lucas was romantic, actually, just not in the traditional sense. And he was right. The flowers would be wilted and dead by lunch. But still, I appreciated Mason's efforts. What I didn't appreciate was watching Monique scurry over to Lucas. She was absolutely too beautiful. I wanted to scrub the freckles off my face.

"So, how are you feeling?" Mason asked, bringing my attention back to him.

"Just a few aches. Nothing to worry about."

"If I'd been through what you went through, I think I'd be ready to call the trip quits."

"Yesterday was kinda like river rafting. There was some excitement to it." Understatement.

"Probably better with a raft, though, don't you think?"

I chuckled. "Yeah."

"So, maybe tonight we can do that candlelit dinner."

I scrunched my nose. "I think Lucas is going to want everyone to stick close to camp."

"He's not our boss."

"He's mine."

"You should consider staying behind with us, once we get to our destination. We could have some fun."

"I know they're going to leave someone behind—"

"So volunteer."

"Maybe." I didn't know how Lucas would feel about it, but the idea had a certain appeal. It might give me a chance to explore the area, to figure out where my parents had died. The problem was that when I was five, all the forest had looked the same to me, and even if it hadn't, it would have changed in the dozen years since I left.

For the following two days we made terrific progress. Lucas always took the lead. We were traveling where no campers had gone before. He had a wicked-looking machete that he used to clear through the brush. He pushed each of us to our personal limit, and when we reached that, he pushed us further. Every night we pretty much collapsed once the campsite was set up. No flirting, no fun.

Dr. Keane seemed pleased with the pace. Once he got to wherever it was he wanted to be, we'd leave him to his business, and return at the end of two weeks to help them haul their stuff back.

There hadn't been any other strange incidents. We were still taking turns keeping guard at night. Lucas was always my partner. We didn't talk. We took opposite sides of the camp. I studied him until he turned his head to look at me—then I shifted my attention away and tried to appear nonchalant, hoping he didn't realize how much time I spent fantasizing about him.

Thoughts about him occupied me as much as memories of the wolf. I heard him howl every night before I drifted off to sleep. I kept expecting him to show up while I was on guard duty. For some reason, I didn't think Lucas would be alarmed by him strolling through camp. Because the howls never sounded far away, I was certain he was following us. That knowledge gave me a sense of security that I couldn't explain.

It was late afternoon on the fourth day since my river incident that we broke through the brush into a gorgeous clearing. It was larger than any we'd reached before. In front of us was a narrow stream, the water babbling as it traveled. It wasn't nearly as ominous as the river we'd crossed before. A short distance away, the land sloped up more steeply, and I knew we were at the base of the mountains. The valley was spread out before us. It was all so peaceful.

"What do you think, Professor?" Lucas asked.

I glanced back to see Dr. Keane nodding. "This will do very nicely, very nicely indeed."

As we set up the camp, I felt a growing sense of accomplishment in knowing that we wouldn't be packing it all back up the next morning. Dr. Keane and his students would be here for about ten days.

The sherpa guys had gone hunting in typical us-Tarzan-you-Jane fashion. They were hoping to snare some rabbits. I was gathering kindling at the edge of the copse of trees when Mason approached.

"Have you given any thought to my suggestion?" he asked. "I really want *you* to stay here with us."

He reached for my hand and then looked confused when he saw they were both filled with kindling. So instead he slid his hand up my forearm and wrapped his fingers around my elbow. "I like you, Kayla. A lot. I mean, more than a lot. I'd like some time to . . . well, to explore what I'm feeling. Maybe find that shooting star."

My whole life—or at least since my parents had died—I'd liked whatever was safe. I'd searched for safe. Lucas wasn't safe. He stirred things in me that I'd never felt before. Scary things. Enormous feelings welled inside me whenever he was around. Sometimes I felt like the girl inside me would crawl out of my skin and I'd become someone totally different if I spent too much time with Lucas.

Lucas was the big, bad wolf, and Mason was the one who'd built the house that the wolf couldn't get into. Mason was a warm blanket on a winter night. Lucas was . . . I didn't know what he was. But he scared the hell out of me.

"I don't know how they decide who stays behind," I told him honestly.

"Volunteer. You can share a tent with Monique."

She wasn't my first choice, but since she was the only girl she was my only choice. I envisioned listening to her talking incessantly every night as we got ready for bed about how hot Lucas was. I thought it might drive me crazy, but on the other hand I could talk about Mason. Besides, I couldn't think of a better way to face my past than to spend a few days out here just living, instead of hiking until I was too exhausted at night to really care about anything.

"I'll ask Lucas."

"Great. I'm really glad you're going to stay."

"I'm going to *try* to stay. We'll have to see what Lucas says."

"I'm not so sure that's a good idea." Lucas had his arms crossed over his chest and his I-am-the-leader-so-you-will-not-mess-with-me scowl, ruining the perfect lines of his face.

"Why?" I asked.

"You're a novice."

"I've camped my entire life. I'll admit I'm not as familiar with these woods as you are, but they're woods like any other woods. The camp is set up. They're going to do a little day hiking and looking around. I don't see that it's a big deal. Besides, you have to cut me loose sometime."

"Why do you want to stay?" he demanded to know.

"For the experience. To face my past—"

"Why?"

"Because Dr. Keane is interesting with all his wild theories, and it might be fun—"

"Why?"

I gritted my teeth. Why was he being so difficult?

"Because I like Mason, okay? I want to spend some time with him, get to know him. I'm comfortable around him." *And I'm not always comfortable around you.*

"Fine. Stay."

His words were terse. Harsh. Filled with anger. I didn't know why I felt let down when he turned on his heel and strode away. I'd gotten what I wanted. More time with Mason. More time where everything was safe.

Why did I feel as though I'd lost something that was more important?

That night when I went to bed, for the first time, I was looking forward to my shift as guardian. Mason had been a little over the top with his excitement about me staying with the group. He even gave me one of their green Keane's Kampers T-shirts to wear—how juvenile. He'd stuck to me like paper to glue. It was so obvious that he was incredibly happy that I was going to be around. It should have made me feel just as glad.

But Lucas was as sullen as Mason was happy. He kept his distance. He and Rafe did a lot of low talking on the other side of the camp. At one point, it looked like they were arguing. Lucas's face took on a stormy expression, and he finally walked away.

"Man, I thought he was going to hit him," Mason whispered beside me, and I realized that I wasn't the only one watching the little drama unfold.

I had a sneaking suspicion they were discussing me and my insistence that I stay behind. But why would Rafe care? For that matter, why would Lucas? We hadn't hooked up or anything.

When Lindsey finally returned to the tent and nudged me with a tired "Your turn," I was more than ready to get out of the tent. I wanted to talk with Lucas, try to explain—

What exactly?

I wasn't sure. I just knew that I didn't want him to leave in the morning still upset with me. But he was the one who'd said he had more important things to worry over than me. Mason made me feel like I was the *only* important thing.

A girl needs that.

But when I stepped out of the tent, it wasn't Lucas waiting for me. It was Connor.

"Where's Lucas?" I asked.

"Asleep, I guess. I'll take that side." He started to walk away.

"Connor?"

He stopped and looked back at me. He wasn't wearing his usual teasing grin. I wanted the reason to be that it was so late, but I knew he was upset with me as well.

"I don't understand why my staying is a big deal."

He sighed. "I know. And that's the reason it's a big deal."

"So why doesn't someone explain it to me?" I gave him a pointed glare.

"It's not my place."

What a lame excuse. "Whatever. It's only ten days. Geez. You guys are acting like I'm betraying you or something."

"We just didn't expect you to be the one to stay. That's all."

Because I was the newbie? If Lucas was really concerned about it, he could have insisted I leave. Things were so confusing. I was grateful I'd have a few days to myself without Lucas bombarding my thoughts.

In typical guy fashion, Connor walked away as though all my questions had been answered. Only I had more questions. But he wasn't going to answer them. I thought about waking Lucas up, but I didn't want to bother him. Especially when he got so little sleep as it was.

And if he was able to sleep, how bothered could he really be about me staying here? Not much.

I walked the perimeter and when I got to the stream, I stood there and watched the moonlight dancing over the water.

It was only then that I realized I hadn't heard the wolf howl that night. I wondered if we'd traveled out of his territory. If we'd left him behind. It made me sad to think so, almost made me consider heading back tomorrow, just to have him closer again.

But that was a silly thought. It was probably all

coincidence anyway—his howling when I went to bed each night.

I was going to have fun here with Mason.

The sherpas left at dawn. As I stood at the edge of the camp and watched them leave, I saw that Lindsey was the only one who looked back. This sense of abandonment was ridiculous. It wasn't like we'd never see each other again.

As for the atmosphere of betrayal, that was even sillier.

I wasn't exactly sure why I'd thought it would be exciting to stay behind. Dr. Keane was a professor, and not to dis academics, but if he taught class with as much enthusiasm as he planned activities in the wild, I never wanted to take one of his classes. I figured everyone slept through it.

For two days, we stayed so close to the camp that I hesitated to call what we were doing hiking. We were near the mountains. There were virgin trails to explore, skills to be tested. But Dr. Keane was constantly checking the gear—a little late for that, since it wasn't as though an REI store was nearby—making notations in his notebook, and looking off into the distance.

After lunch on the third day, I went up to Mason and said, "We need to make a break for it."

He grinned. "Yeah, my dad is a little controlling—and he can be sort of unimaginative. What'd you have in mind?"

"Exploring the mountains."

"Let's do it."

Even though it was early afternoon and we wouldn't be going too far, I grabbed my backpack.

Hiking with Mason was way different from hiking with Lucas. I told myself it was because we didn't have any particular goal to be reached, whereas Lucas always had a goal. But Mason didn't lead. Instead we just walked side by side.

"So, do you know where you're going to college?" he asked.

"Thought I'd start out at the community college. No SATs, ACTs, or any kind of Ts needed to get into the one at home." I gave him a rueful smile. "I suck at tests."

He grinned. "Me, too. Even when I study my butt off. Soon as they say to take out that number two pencil or that blue book—game over, man. Needless to say, it doesn't endear me to dear old Dad."

Today was the first time I'd heard him say anything even remotely derogatory about his father. "You and your dad seem to get along." Well, except for the night that they'd talked about werewolves.

"Yeah, usually we do, but when you get right down to

it, he's still a parent. He doesn't always remember what it's like to be young."

"I hear you."

The shadows had begun lengthening. I was surprised by how much progress we'd made. We were away from everything and everyone, except the wilderness.

"We should probably turn back," I suggested.

"Not yet." He reached into one of his pants pockets and pulled out a thick white candle. "I promised you dinner by candlelight."

"But if we have it here and now, we'll risk losing the light and our way back to camp. It's really not wise—"

"Wise, schmize. So we won't do dinner. Let's at least do a snack by candlelight."

It sounded a lot more romantic than I thought it would probably be, but what the heck? It was more romance than Lucas had ever given me. Also, I was irritated that three days later, I was still thinking about him. Without all the equipment to haul and the inexperienced hikers to slow them down, he and the others were probably already back at the village preparing to take another group into the wilderness before returning for us.

Mason and I shrugged out of our backpacks. It felt great to get the weight off my shoulders. I did a couple of stretches. Mason balanced the candle on an empty tin can. He turned back to his backpack. "Go ahead and sit down. I just have a couple more things to set up."

I sat cross-legged on the ground. "You know, I don't know if lighting the candle is really a good idea. It's not exactly steady, and I'd hate to make the national news as the romantic couple who accidentally burned five million acres of forest land."

"You're probably right," he answered, clearly distracted.

I tried to lean around him. "What are you doing?"

He swung back around and sat down beside me. "Nothing."

"I'm glad you asked me to hang around," I told him.

"It really means a lot to me that you stayed." He touched my cheek. "I'd never hurt you."

"That's kind of an odd thing to say."

"I haven't dated that much. All the academics, you know? Guess I'm a loser in that regard."

"Don't be silly. I mean, what does it say about me if you're a loser?"

"Right, yeah. I really like you, Kayla." Then he leaned in and kissed me.

But it wasn't gentle or sweet. It was so un-Mason-like, rough, almost desperate, that I pushed him away.

He pushed back—hard. I hit the ground. He straddled me. "I'm sorry," he whispered low. He started kissing me again. Rougher than before.

Panic surged through me. What was he doing? Why was he doing it? Until this moment he'd been so nice.

I started slapping at him. He grabbed my wrists with one hand and held them above my head. He lowered his mouth near my ear.

"Just go along with it," he said in a low voice.

"No! Get off!"

I shook my head from side to side, trying to break free, but he clamped his free hand on my jaw and tried to kiss me again. I fought to buck him.

My heart was pounding insanely. I'd never been so terrified, never felt so helpless.

Then I heard it. The low, warning growl. Mason went completely still, his lips only an inch from mine. Strangely, I saw satisfaction ease over his face. I shifted my eyes to the side.

And there was my wolf. He bared his teeth in a menacing snarl.

Mason rolled off me. He scrambled back, and I scooted away.

Suddenly, there was a muffled pop. The wolf released a yelp and staggered.

I looked back. Mason was holding a pistol, aiming it at the wolf.

"No!" I screamed. I lunged—too late.

The wolf leaped. Mason fired again and the wolf went down.

ELEVEN

"Are you insane?" I yelled as I rushed over to the wolf. I couldn't believe what had just happened—any of it.

The wolf wasn't dead, but his beautiful silver eyes had a glazed look to them. He was panting. He made a futile effort to rise and slumped back down. I buried my fingers in his fur, searching for the wounds. I saw only a trickle of blood and realized Mason hadn't been shooting bullets, but darts.

"Got him," I heard him say.

I snapped my head back around. He was holding a walkie-talkie. He strolled over and crouched down beside me. "He's not hurt, just drugged."

I slammed my fist into his shoulder, then punched him in the chest. "You creep!"

"Hey!" he yelled and grabbed my hands. "Take it easy. I wasn't really going to hurt you over there. I just needed him to think that."

I jerked free and shoved him again. I wanted to rip his eyes out for terrifying me.

"Hey, will you stop?" he yelled, scrambling back. "God, I wasn't going to do anything. I was just pretending. I needed him to think you were in danger."

"What are you talking about?"

"I knew he'd show himself if you were being attacked."

Was he insane? Did he think the wolf's personal mission in life was to protect me? I mean, sure, maybe we'd bonded a little with the bear attack, but he was a wild animal, not a domesticated dog. That he was following me, that he'd come to my rescue again—no one could have predicted that. It was just a huge coincidence. While I was stunned by the wolf's presence, I was furious with Mason's actions and betrayals.

"So this whole romancing thing was a ploy to attract the wolf?" I didn't bother to keep the anger out of my voice. His actions were unacceptable. To frighten me, to make me think he was going to hurt me . . . to use me as bait. It was dehumanizing.

"Don't say it as though my feelings for you are insincere," Mason said cajolingly. "I *do* like you, Kayla. A lot. But we had something larger to accomplish and we needed you to be part of it."

I was so angry that I could barely see straight. I felt as though Mason had made a fool of me. But worse, he'd used me, used me to capture the wolf. My voice was seething when I asked, "Mason, what is going on?"

But he wasn't looking at me. He was mesmerized by the wolf. "Look how big he is. Look at how human his eyes are. Everything else changes but the eyes remain human. It's just like he told me it would be."

"Who? What in the hell are you talking about?"

Before he could answer, I heard the crackle of brush being trampled. Coming from between the trees, Ethan and Tyler carried a cage with metal bars. It was a little smaller than the crate they'd been hauling. Was that what had been inside it?

Dr. Keane was behind them. He strode forward and slapped Mason on the back. "Good job, son."

"Thanks, Dad."

As they slipped a muzzle over his mouth, the wolf made another valiant effort to rise.

"I gave him two doses of tranquilizer. He should be knocked out cold with that much," Mason said, clearly baffled. "Should I shoot him again?"

"No, he's drugged enough that we can handle him. His resistance is strong. That's good," Dr. Keane murmured. "He'll need all the strength he has."

I got right in Dr. Keane's face and stood on my toes so he could see how angry I was. "What are you going to do to him?"

Dr. Keane looked at me as though I were an irritating gnat. "Why, study him, of course."

My heart was thundering as I trudged back to camp. I felt as though I'd betrayed the wolf. I thought about how protective Lucas was of the wilderness, the animals, and especially the wolves. I hoped he never found out about this. I could think of only one way to make this right. I had to figure out a way to set the wolf free.

Ethan and Tyler set the cage up at the far end of the campsite, near the woods. An insane excitement reverberated through the camp as everyone came around to stare at the wolf. I hated that he was on display like that. I wondered if animals felt humiliation. Even if he didn't, I was embarrassed for him. He seemed like such a proud creature. He deserved better treatment than this. My heart ached for him.

After a while, everyone wandered off. Everyone except Mason and me. Mason was incredibly fascinated by the wolf. But how could he do this to so beautiful a creature? It wasn't right. I'd thought I knew Mason, but I realized I didn't know him at all. Why hadn't I left with Lucas and the others? And what was I going to do now? They had put a simple key-lock on the cage door. But I didn't think they'd leave the wolf unguarded.

"Isn't it gorgeous?" Mason said, without taking his eyes off the wolf.

My therapist had hypnotized me once to try to get to the root of my fears. I had a feeling I'd looked a lot like Mason did now—like I'd been smoking something illegal.

I was furious with Mason and myself. Why hadn't I seen this coming? There weren't many wolves with this unique shading of fur. I knew it was the one that had saved me from the bear attack. I *owed* this animal. And because of me, he was locked in a cage.

The wolf stirred. I watched as he struggled to his feet. The cage was small. He couldn't stand up fully. He couldn't pace. He would be hard-pressed to turn around. They'd removed the muzzle once they'd gotten him into the cage. I looked into those silver eyes and I felt the same connection I'd felt right after the bear attack. What was there for Dr. Keane to study? He was probably a descendant of the wolves that had been reintroduced into the wild. I had a feeling the wolves' tendency not to attack man was about to be turned around. Dr. Keane and his students were declaring war on a species. Why were they doing this?

Mason crouched, poked a stick through the bars, and jabbed the wolf in his side. He issued a low, warning growl and drew back his lips to show his teeth.

I grabbed the stick from Mason and tossed it aside. I was seething with anger. "Don't do that."

Mason stood up. "You're right. If he's angry, he won't shift back."

"Shift? What are you talking about? He's a wolf and it's illegal to capture them."

He gave me a grin that seemed to say, *What world do you live in?*

"It's not a *wolf*," he said. "Well, obviously it's a wolf right now, but before it shifted, it was human. With that fur coloring, I'm pretty sure it's Lucas. Makes sense. The way he watched you, I knew he wouldn't leave you behind."

Okay, someone needs to go back on his meds. I laughed. "Are you freaking mental?"

He narrowed his eyes at me. "Lycanthropes exist, Kayla. Here, in this wilderness. There's a whole village—"

"No, they don't," I interrupted. "And no, there's not. If anything, it's just legend, crazy stories people tell around the campfire."

With a wicked grin, he leaned toward me. "I can prove it's true."

He crouched down, unzipped his backpack, and removed

a gun. It wasn't like the one he'd used before. This one looked like the Glock my dad carried.

"What the hell—"

Before I finished my sentence, he calmly aimed it at the wolf—

"No!" I screamed, lunging for Mason. Again, too late.

He pulled the trigger. The wolf yelped and fell to his side. Blood gushed from his hip.

Students started rushing over.

"It's okay. Just an accident. The gun misfired. No big deal," Mason called out, waving them back.

No big deal? He'd purposely shot the wolf!

I shoved him hard and he staggered back. "What is wrong with you?" I demanded to know.

"I'm proving my point."

"You *are* mental." If I could get my hands on that gun, I'd shoot him. I grabbed the lock and rattled it. The wolf was panting. I could see the pain in his eyes. "Get this open so I can do something for him, before he bleeds to death."

"Calm down. He's not going to bleed to death."

"Don't tell me to calm down. I'm not going to let you hurt him again. I need to see the wound."

He gave me the calm smile that I was starting to hate. "Okay," he said, crouching. "Look."

I dropped to my knees and curled my hands around two of the bars.

"Look at his hind leg where I shot him," Mason said.

Almost as quickly as the blood had gushed, it began to slow to a drizzle. Then it stopped altogether. Using another stick, Mason lifted the fur. The wound was closing, like a time-lapse video that I'd seen in biology class. I wouldn't have believed it if I hadn't seen it with my own eyes.

"When they're in wolf form, they heal faster than we do," Mason said. "Imagine the medical ramifications. If we can isolate the gene, we can create a serum that would replicate the rapid cell rejuvenation. Someone is in a devastating car wreck, bleeding to death. We give him an injection and he's healed before an ambulance gets him to the nearest hospital. Then, of course, there are the military uses. An army of shape-shifting soldiers, with their heightened sense of smell, hearing, and sight. It would be invincible."

He made it sound as though he were doing all this for the good of mankind. Did it make me an awful human being because I thought it was wrong to exploit this species like that? Not that I believed for one minute that it was a werewolf—that it was Lucas. For some reason, this particular wolf had amazing healing properties—but it had to be a genetic mutation, a fluke. It wasn't a special species of humans who changed into wolves, or wolves that changed into humans.

Mason looked at me. "Of course, the real money will be in recreational uses. If we can create a drug that will transform you for just a couple of hours—wouldn't you take it? Just to know what it's like? Lycanthrope parties will be all the rage. And we'll hold the patent. And if the FDA doesn't approve it—who cares? We'll make more money on the black market anyway."

So it wasn't about the good of mankind. It was about money.

"It was really selfish of you to hold back, Lucas. You should have willingly donated yourself to our research. Instead we had to come out here and lure you into our trap. It was so easy once we realized how protective you were of Kayla." Mason poked him again, and the wolf growled.

"It's not Lucas. You sound insane," I insisted.

"Of course it is. You'll see. He'll grow too weak to hold this shape, and he'll revert back to human form. Then you'll know."

"They're not going to let you walk out of here with a wolf."

He gave me a cocky grin. "We're not walking. We have choppers landing in the morning. Why do you think we wanted a spot at the edge of a large valley? We'll take you with us, and once you see everything, you'll understand the significance of our work. I want you to be part of it. We'll have that candlelit dinner to celebrate."

In my mind I was screaming, "No way!"

But I knew I had to play it cool. Until I could figure out a strategy of escape for me and the wolf, I had to start pretending that I thought all this was amazing. I had to lie. And I needed more information.

"So what? You're taking him back to the university?"

"God, Kayla, how naïve can you be? Get with the program. It was all a con. My dad isn't a professor. He's head of research at Bio-Chrome. Ever heard of us? 'Studying chromosomes for a better tomorrow'?"

I had a vague recollection of some stupid commercial I'd seen on TV.

"But his students—"

"We're all his research team. We're geniuses." He laughed. "I graduated from college at seventeen. My roommate used to live around here. He told me about the rumors that shape-shifters were hiding in this forest. Even told me to keep a special eye on Lucas. I started doing research. Way too many sightings for it not to be true. And now we'll not only prove it, but we'll benefit from it." He looked back at the wolf. "You're going to make history, Lucas."

Mason turned his attention back to me. "Can you envision it? Can you see what we're going to accomplish?

I want you to be part of it, Kayla. We want you to be part of the team."

"I'm still in high school, Mason," I said, playing along. There was no way I was going to join his team.

He rolled his eyes. "This is a once-in-a-lifetime opportunity, Kayla. My dad can get you a high school equivalency diploma. You can start taking college courses online while you work on the research. This will all be cutting-edge. We'll all be millionaires. We're offering you an opportunity to be part of it."

I swallowed hard. "It sounds great," I lied. "I'm so in."

"I knew you would be once you understood everything. And don't worry about Lucas. He'll come to understand it all, too."

Mason got up and walked away, leaving me there. My fingers were wrapped so tightly around the bars that they were beginning to ache. I studied the wolf and held his gaze. He held mine.

It was a strange connection. Maybe I was a little insane, too. I knew werewolves—shift-shapers, lycanthropes, whatever you wanted to call them—existed only in movies and TV shows. Still, I leaned near and whispered, "Lucas?"

With great effort, he lifted his head and licked my fingers.

I released my hold on the bars and scrambled back. It couldn't be. It just couldn't be. Werewolves did *not* exist.

And this wasn't Lucas.

I jerked my head up at the sound of someone approaching. Ethan was holding a rifle. I didn't know if it held more tranquilizer darts or bullets. He gave me an awkward smile.

"Pretty cool, huh?" he asked. He sat on the ground, leaned against a tree, and set the rifle on his lap.

"Are you afraid he's going to stage a prison break?" I asked lightly, trying to appear as nonthreatening as possible.

He shrugged. "Until we study him, we don't know what he's capable of. Besides, he's not the only one. The others might try something."

This was just getting better and better.

I was furious at Mason and his father, and I was terrified for the wolf. I was plotting an escape. But I knew none of that showed on my face as I sat by the campfire following supper. Mason was toasting marshmallows again, which seemed so bizarre. Dr. Keane was sitting on his little stool. I envisioned kicking it out from beneath him and laughing as he tumbled to the ground. But he wasn't worth my effort.

I had to act normal. I had to give them the impression that I'd accepted their insane plan and that I could be trusted.

Mason offered me his perfect marshmallow. I gave him

a flirtatious smile before popping it into my mouth.

"See, Dad?" Mason said. "I told you once she understood, she'd see the value in our work."

Dr. Keane gave me a suspicious look, so I smiled brightly and said, "I think you're an absolute genius."

Dr. Keane's chest puffed out slightly and he yammered on for a while about all the money they'd make once they figured out the werewolves' secret to transforming.

"So you think there are more creatures like this one?" I asked, pretending to be interested in his insane ideas.

"Oh, absolutely," Dr. Keane said.

I glanced over at the cage. Tyler was standing guard over it now. "Shouldn't you feed him? Or at least give him some water? You wouldn't want him to die on you."

"Oh, I think he's a long way from dying. Right now it's imperative that we weaken him, so he'll revert to human form. Takes a lot of energy to stay in wolf form," said Evil Scientist—my new name for Dr. Keane.

"How can you even know that?" I asked.

"Because it makes sense."

"What if the wolf form is his natural form and it takes more energy to remain in human form?" I asked. I'd been trying to make conversation, but the words sent a chill through me. I didn't believe any of their insane theories, but what if they were true? Would it be cool to be able to shift into another shape? Or would it be a nightmare? A nightmare, I decided. Ever since my parents were killed, I'd spent my life trying to fit in. I couldn't imagine anything more horrifying than being so different from everyone else.

Evil Scientist pondered my question for a moment, then smiled his wicked evil-scientist grin. "I guess we'll do some experiments and figure it out. Which came first? The wolf or the human?"

I wished I'd kept my mouth shut. I didn't want them experimenting on the wolf. I felt an obligation to protect him.

Mason took my hand. "Don't look so worried. It's not to our benefit to hurt him."

Right. And shooting him was your way of making him feel good.

I didn't say anything aloud. I just plastered on a smile that said, "I think you're absolutely wonderful. Great boyfriend material. I'm the luckiest girl."

"The chopper will be here at dawn," Dr. Keane said. "We'll need to break camp before that. We probably all need to turn in early."

As everyone got up and headed toward the tents, Mason took my hand again and pulled me into the shadows. "I just want you to know that I wanted you to stay here because I do like you. It wasn't just about using you to capture the werewolf."

"You could have just told me. Then I could have helped."

"We needed your reaction to be honest." He touched my cheek. "I really like you, Kayla."

I smiled. "I like you, too." The lie came easily, maybe because he'd told me so many lies that I didn't have any problem repeating a few back to him.

He leaned in to kiss me. I put my hand on his chest. I couldn't bear the thought of him kissing me. "I'm sorry. After this afternoon, I'm a little bruised—physically and emotionally. Even though I understand why you did what you did, and I would have done the same in your place, I'd like to go a little slow now."

"Sure. You're right. It's been a day of discovery."

A day of betrayal was what I was thinking.

He walked me to my tent and said goodnight. I crawled into the tent I was sharing with Monique. She was already curled up in her sleeping bag and reading a book.

"So all the flirting you were doing with Lucas . . .?"

She smiled. "Just part of the lure. Although he is hot. And if he is this wolf, that makes him so much hotter."

She was sick. Totally.

As I got ready for bed, I slipped my metal nail file out of my backpack and tucked it into the pocket of my shorts. I would need it to pick the lock.

It may seem strange, but after all, my adoptive dad is a

cop. I was bound to pick up a few tips on criminal activities like hotwiring cars and breaking and entering.

I made my way into my sleeping bag. "Goodnight."

It was several minutes before Monique turned out the light. I lay there, not moving, just planning.

I finally heard Monique's breathing drop into that slow shallow rhythm that meant she'd gone to sleep. I hadn't zipped my sleeping bag because I hadn't wanted the rasp of the zipper to wake her up. I scooted out from my bag. Looking over my shoulder at her, I tugged on my boots. A bright moon provided enough light for me to see her silhouette. She didn't move at all. I slipped my hand back into my sleeping bag and wrapped my fingers around my flashlight. I always kept it handy in case I had to get up in the middle of the night. I definitely needed it tonight.

I crept out of the tent. I didn't take my backpack with me. I wasn't planning to leave—I didn't think I could make it back to the village on my own anyway. I just wanted to set the wolf free. If Mason and his dad figured out it was me, they might get mad, but they weren't going to shoot me. Would they? Of course not. I did think they'd gone over to the dark side, but they were scientists, not murderers.

The camp was eerily quiet. I straightened and slipped around behind the tent. I moved stealthily until I reached the outer perimeter where Ethan was once again watching the cage. He was sitting cross-legged. Every now and then, he poked the wolf with a sharp stick. I guess he figured if he wasn't getting any sleep, the wolf shouldn't either. Or maybe it was part of their plan to wear the wolf down until he shifted back into human form. Personally, I thought it was a bad idea to prod wild creatures.

I tightened my hold on the flashlight. It was a good, heavy, solid tool. When needed, it made a terrific club. And right now I needed a club.

My heart was pounding so hard that I was surprised the guy didn't hear it. Actually, I was surprised it didn't wake the entire camp. I took another step—

Snap!

I landed on a dry twig and grimaced. Ethan started to twist around—

I swung with everything I had in me. The flashlight slammed against his skull. I felt the shock of the contact ricochet up my arm. Ethan keeled over in a sprawl. He never even saw me. I knelt beside him and checked his pulse. It was steady. He probably wouldn't be out for long. I had to work fast.

I took a quick look around. I couldn't believe they had only one person guarding their precious prize, but I figured they thought he was securely locked up. And only Evil Scientist had the key.

I scrambled around to the door, turned on my flashlight,

and set it so the light illuminated the padlock. It wasn't anything fancy. This was going to be easy. I pulled the file from my pocket and went to work.

"I'll have you out of here in a minute," I whispered.

I was surprised by how alert the wolf seemed. Especially since they'd been denying him any sort of comfort or essentials—like food and water—while trying to weaken him. Sadists.

He issued a low growl, almost a purr. A throaty sound. I ignored it. I didn't want him trying to communicate with me. I just wanted him to get the hell away.

I heard the lock click. I snapped it apart and jerked open the door. Swallowing hard, I scooted back.

With lithe movements, the wolf sauntered out of the cage and went over to the guard. He began sniffing around. I wondered if he was considering eating him.

I moved over to him. "No!" I hissed. "You have to go. Shoo! Go!"

But he didn't go. He just got very, very still, unnaturally so, and I could feel a small electric charge in the air. I stood up and glanced around. We were still lucky. No one was in sight. Maybe if I hit the wolf with my flashlight, it would frighten him away. I reached down, grabbed it from where I'd left it on the ground, and turned back—

The wolf was gone. But I felt no relief. As a matter of fact, I felt close to panic. Because while the wolf was no longer there, Lucas was.

A very naked Lucas was crouched near Ethan. I couldn't process that. *He was a werewolf? Dr. Keane and Mason were right? No, no, no.* There was another explanation. There had to be. My world tilted and I had an urge to scream hysterically.

I stared at his bare back while he tugged off Ethan's cargo pants. He had absolutely no tan lines. He was like a perfect bronzed god. I might have fallen in lust right then and there if I didn't know that he came with issues in the form of a furry body and canine incisors.

"Good luck," I said. My voice quivered, and I knew I sounded completely dazed. I was close to totally losing it. Maybe I was still in my tent dreaming. I took a step back toward the shadows.

"Wait!" Lucas ordered in a low voice.

I glanced back. He'd already pulled on the pants and was zipping them up.

"I have to go," I said.

Before I could race away, he was beside me, grabbing my arm.

I jerked away. "Leave me alone. You're free. Just go."

"I'm not leaving you here with Mason. Not after what he tried to do to you—"

"It was all fake. He wasn't going to hurt me." I shook my head. "I don't know how or why, but he knew you

163

were around and he was trying to draw you out. Obviously it worked."

He clenched his jaw. "I fell right into his trap. I forgot about everything when he attacked you. I just wanted to rip his throat out. He might try it again—"

"No, I'm on to him now. I won't let him put me in that position." As a matter of fact, I was thinking that I might head out on my own as soon as I saw that Lucas was safely gone.

"You have to come with me," Lucas said.

"I'll be fine."

"No. You won't be," he said with incredible seriousness. But then he was always serious. The guy never laughed, and he seldom smiled. But, oh, when he smiled, the things it did to my heart.

"They don't know it was me who let you out," I insisted.

"That doesn't matter. In less than forty-eight hours there will be a full moon, the first full moon since your birthday."

"So?"

"The first transformation happens during the first full moon after your seventeenth birthday."

"Okay, great, nice to know, but we don't have time for a *Werewolves for Dummies* lesson. You need to get out of here."

I should have run when he stepped over to me, but I

didn't. I stood there gazing into his silver eyes. They held me captive. They wouldn't let me look away. I felt this strange pull. I wanted to lean into him. I wanted to wrap myself around him. Around Lucas, who always made me feel like I wanted to crawl out of my skin. His eyes were so solemn. But there was something else there, something possessive.

I wanted this to be a romantic moment, like those corny movies. I wanted him to take me in his arms and kiss me like his life depended on it. Then I wanted him to run off into the woods and disappear forever. Be safe.

Why was it suddenly so important to me that he be safe?

He wrapped his hands around my arms. I thought he would jerk me toward him now and plant that kiss that I so desperately wanted.

Instead he said solemnly, "Kayla, you're one of us."

TWELVE

For such a little word, *us* had huge ramifications. *Us* could mean the human race. Well, except that he wasn't human, not totally. Or at least, I didn't think he was.

It could mean that since I'd rescued him, I was now destined to follow him around. In some cultures, when a person saved someone's life, they were tied together forever. I'd read that somewhere. My babbling mind was searching for other explanations for *us*. Maybe it meant . . .

God, who was I kidding here? There was only one thing that it could mean and it wasn't what I wanted it to mean. *Us*. Whatever he was, he was including me in that little circle of weirdness. It wasn't natural. People did not turn into wolves. I had enough freakish baggage to deal with. I was not going to add being physically abnormal to the list.

Ethan moaned.

Lucas took my hand. "Come on, we gotta go before he sounds the alarm."

I shook my head. "I'm not like you."

"We'll discuss it later. We have to go."

"I'm not going."

"Kayla, in less than forty-eight hours they'll know the truth about you, then you'll be the one in the cage. If you survive the transformation. You need me to help you do that . . . *if* you want to survive."

This was just getting better and better. Not only was he saying that I was going to go all furry, but . . . I might die in the process if he wasn't there? My mind was trying to process this, and it just wouldn't. I was human. I was not like him. And *us*? How many of *us* were there? I couldn't make sense of any of this. I just couldn't understand it. It was too large to comprehend. My mind wanted to shut down.

There really were people who could transform into wolves? And I was one of them?

The whole idea was totally out of control.

Ethan groaned louder and started struggling to get up. Lucas and I were back in the shadows, but it wouldn't be long until Ethan was aware of us.

Lucas apparently had reached the end of his patience, because he dipped down, picked me up, and slung me over his shoulder. Before I could even catch my breath to voice a protest, he was running. Fast. His feet, as always, were silent.

How could he be so strong, so quick, so quiet when I was draped over his shoulder? What was he? Superwolf?

I was still clutching my flashlight. I thought about swinging it between his legs. That would stop him and dump me on the ground at the same time. But I didn't. I just hung there with trees rushing by in a blur.

You're one of us.

I'm one of them.

I thought about this strange fear that had been circling inside me—the fear with origins I couldn't figure out. I considered all the strange inner sensations I'd had, the feeling that I was changing in ways I couldn't comprehend.

I told myself they were normal teenage fears, normal teenage changes.

I wasn't one of *them*. Lucas was wrong. Maybe he wanted me to be like him.

But he was mistaken. I wasn't like him. I was normal. I was Kayla Madison, confused teenage girl.

I was not about to become a werewolf.

* * *

I don't know how long or how far Lucas ran before I finally yelled, "Okay already, stop!"

He didn't listen. He just kept going.

I hit his butt with my flashlight. "Stop! I mean it! Stop or I'll—"

I'll what? He's bigger, tougher, stronger.

Maybe he heard something in my voice, or maybe he was just worn out, but he came to a halt and let me down. My feet hit the earth, but my legs were wobbly and I collapsed onto the ground.

He crouched beside me. He was breathing heavily, like I did when I ran up stairs. But it seemed like after all that running with me over his shoulder, he should be panting, gasping. I'd never in a million years be so in shape.

The moonlight was breaking through the branches, but I wanted more. I wanted sunlight, but it wouldn't be here for a few more hours. I turned on my flashlight. I didn't shine it directly into his face. I didn't need to. Just having it on was enough.

"You didn't run into anything," I said. It was a mindless thing to say. I guess he thought so, too, because he looked a little surprised.

"I have really good night vision," he finally said.

"Is that because you're a—"

"Yeah. Vision, hearing, smell—they all improve after the first transformation."

I nodded and swallowed. "So what are you . . . exactly?"

"Technical term is lycanthrope. We refer to ourselves as Shifters. People who don't know any better call us werewolves." He glanced around. "We need to start walking, put more distance between us and the Statics."

"Statics?" I asked.

"Those who never change." He said it with a hint of sadness. I didn't know if he was feeling sorry for those who didn't have the ability to shift or those who did.

He took my hand and pulled me to my feet. I swayed. If I hadn't knocked against him, I probably would have hit the ground again. His arms came around me and he held my gaze. "I know it's a shock, everything you've learned tonight."

Ya think? I shook my head, then nodded. I was still so confused. My brain wasn't firing on all cylinders. "What did you mean when you said 'if I wanted to survive'?"

Gently, he touched my cheek with his fingertips. They were rough and callused. I didn't want to think that earlier in the night they'd also sported claws that could rip my face apart. "The first time you shift it's painful, like childbirth. In a way, I guess that makes sense. You're giving birth to your inner wolf. So you need your mate there to coach you through it."

"My mate?" *Is he for real?*

"Don't you feel it?" he asked. "This pull between us?"

Was he talking about this thing that terrified me?

I stepped away from him. "I don't want this!" I stalked around in the little bit of area we had between the trees. "I didn't ask for this!" I came to an abrupt halt. "So what? At some point in my life I was bitten?"

"It's genetic, just like Keane said."

"You're saying that I inherited this ability to shift? What? Like from my parents? That they were"—I stuttered and stopped, trying to wrap my mind around the ramifications—"that they were wolves?"

He just looked at me.

"That's insane! They would have told me." I had this flash memory of wolves. I ignored it. "And you're wrong. I'm not one of you."

His large shoulders rolled into a shrug. "Okay, you're not. But you'd better stick with me—just in case I'm right. Besides, Evil Scientist will know you helped me escape and he's not very forgiving."

My brow furrowed so deeply that it hurt. "How did you know that I call him that?" I backed up a step. "Oh my God! You can read minds?" My voice shimmered with outrage and accusation. He didn't bother to deny it. Did he know everything I thought?

"Only when I'm in wolf form," he said. He took the flashlight, clicked it off, and handed it back to me. "No sense in broadcasting where we're going."

He grabbed my hand and tugged me deeper into the woods. I didn't want to go, but he was right. Unfortunately. I was stuck with him until I could figure out my alternatives.

My eyes adjusted to the wilderness bathed in moonlight. I was following so closely behind Lucas that I pretty much stepped where he stepped. His hand held mine firmly. He was so tall and broad, and his fingers felt so strong wrapped around mine, that I wondered if he was naturally this way or if it came about when he first shifted into wolf form. Of course, I guessed that *naturally* was the wrong word. On the other hand, for him shifting was natural. *Not* to shift was weird.

It was an upside-down, insane world that I was suddenly part of.

I had a gazillion questions, but since we were trying to be quiet until we reached wherever we were going— I hadn't asked and he hadn't said, but his strides definitely had a purpose—I kept all my questions to myself. Besides, he was moving fast and I was having a difficult time keeping pace. I had thought I was in decent shape, but I was breathing like a dog after it chased a Frisbee. Dog, wolf—I needed to stop thinking about animals.

I didn't have a lot of time left to figure out how not to

shift into a wild creature—if I truly was about to shift. I still had doubts about that. Wouldn't you *know*, deep down, if you were part wolf or had any bit of wolf in you? It just all seemed inconceivable. But if it was about to happen, surely there was some way to prevent it. If I fought it . . . mind over matter. Or in this case, mind over wolf. I just wouldn't accept it.

Because if I accepted it, did I have to accept Lucas as my mate? Shouldn't I have a choice in the matter?

He'd asked if I felt the pull. I couldn't deny that I did. And that it terrified me.

It wasn't like a crush. It wasn't like seeing a guy and thinking I'd like him to take me to the prom. It was soul-deep, as though he was everything, the one, forever. I had to remind myself that I barely knew the guy. But still I couldn't shake the feeling of being meant for each other—as corny as that sounded.

We were going into a part of the wilderness that I'd never been to before. The brush was thick, the trees growing closely together. The thick canopy overhead nearly blocked out every drop of moonlight. He was dragging me up an incline and then stopping me from skidding down on the other side.

I remembered that he was barefoot. His feet would be a bloodied mess of scrapes and cuts. He never complained. He never grunted. He just kept going as though the hounds of hell were on our tail.

Only *he* was the hound of hell.

I was completely lost. My movements were robotic, made without thought.

Eventually we were scrambling up the side of a rocky, forested slope. I knew instinctively that Lucas could have shifted and been far away by now. He could have traversed the rugged terrain easily. Instead, he had to keep reaching back for me.

"You should go on," I insisted after sliding down a couple of feet and skinning my elbows.

"I'm not leaving you."

"But you're the one in the most danger. They won't harm me."

He stopped and gave me a hard look over his shoulder. "I'm not leaving you, Kayla."

Stubborn. So what if Mason and his "friends" found me? They'd just keep trailing after Lucas, and I could drift away. But it was obvious that Lucas wasn't going to listen. I put some extra muscle into my efforts.

When I finally caught up to him, he said, "Okay, just keep climbing. I'm going back to erase our trail. I won't be gone long."

In a panic, I grabbed his arm. "You'll lose me."

"I can track your scent."

"Really? Do you need to take a piece of my clothing or

something, to remind you?"

"No, but—" He leaned in against my throat. I heard him inhale. "You smell so good. I'd find you anywhere."

Was that his idea of romance? I couldn't deny that it did warm me. Before I could respond, he was gone.

I wanted to sit down and think about all this. I wanted to try to make sense of it. Everything had started to get weird after the river. Maybe I'd really drowned. Maybe I was in hell. But that didn't make sense either. What I did know was that Lucas was in danger and if I didn't start moving, Keane and his group might catch up with us. I wasn't worried about me. I wasn't the one they wanted to study. But I didn't want anything to happen to Lucas.

My worries for him gave an urgency to my movements. I was determined not to be the reason that he ended up back in that cage. Being studied, like an animal in a lab. An *animal*. That word resounded in my head. When I looked at Lucas now, I saw a human who transformed into a wolf. Mason and his dad saw a wolf. They didn't see the human anymore, the person. They saw only the unusual creature whose existence defied logic.

Their view of him justified putting him in a cage. My view had compelled me to set him free.

I slipped, caught hold of a sapling, and clung to it, catching my breath while trying to figure out how I could go farther. Everything suddenly seemed crammed together. Small crevices and rocks. Which way would keep him safe?

"You made better progress than I expected," he said as he approached me.

I nearly screamed at the unexpectedness of his arrival. He needed to wear a collar with bells or something so I'd hear him approaching.

He sat beside me. "You okay?"

I nodded. "Just taking a minute to catch my breath."

"It gets harder from here," he said.

"Oh, great."

"But I have a plan." He got up, moved away, and ducked behind some brush.

"What are you—" Something landed on my face. I pulled it away. His pants. "Uh, Lucas?"

"It's okay. I'm going to shift. I'm more surefooted as a wolf. You'll climb on my back, and we'll make better time."

"You're not a horse."

"Trust me. This is the only way to get where we need to be."

I couldn't see him clearly. "I do trust—"

He was gone and the wolf stepped out.

"We should take this show to Vegas," I mumbled.

He released a tiny growl that sounded more like a chuckle. Could wolves laugh?

176

He nudged my thigh.

"I don't think I can."

He licked my hand.

"Oh, okay, when you put it that way." I tied the pants around my waist. I straddled Lucas and dug my fingers into his fur to hang on. I bent my legs back and put my feet on his backside so they weren't dragging the ground. I clung to him when he started moving. I could feel his muscles bunching and stretching beneath me. He was so powerful. I wondered if I would be as well. Did he work out or was his physique related to his genes? He had such a hot bod—

I shut down the thought, remembering that when he was in this form, he could read my thoughts. I worked to make my mind go blank. It was an invasion of privacy, this ability he had, and we were going to have to set up parameters, but until we did, I started mentally arranging the shoes in my closet back home. My mom was a shoe-aholic, so I had at least fifty pairs that I could think about while Lucas clambered over uneven terrain. We went through narrow crevices. Eventually he stopped and gave his body a little shake. I climbed off him. He wandered over to a bush and went behind it.

"Throw me my pants," he said, standing up so his head and shoulders were visible.

"You do that really fast." I tossed him the pants.

"You will, too, once you get used to it and learn the tricks."

Number one: I'd never get used to it. Number two: I wasn't convinced I was going to go furry. Number three: I didn't want to learn any tricks.

Lucas came out from behind the bush. "Shoes? You really own that many pairs of shoes?"

I released a self-conscious laugh. "Can you turn that off? Getting inside my head?"

"There's a way to mute your thoughts. I'll teach you."

"Good, because it wouldn't be fair if you knew everything I was thinking but you were screening your thoughts from me."

"There isn't anything I'd think that I wouldn't want you to know." He took my hand again. "It's just a little farther."

We went down a little bit and took a turn. In the distance I could hear the rushing of water.

I stumbled over something, lost my balance—

Lucas caught me before I could do a face-plant. How did he move so fast? If he was right about me, would I have reflexes that quick? Did I want them?

"Almost there," he said as he helped me to regain my balance.

"Where's 'there'?"

"A hiding place."

When I thought of a hiding place, I thought of some-place small and dark. A place where you crouched and quaked. I wasn't looking forward to it. Especially since I'd be cramped into and nestled right up against Lucas. Would I be able to resist my urges?

We stepped out of the woods and into a small clearing. Moonlight spilled around us. The rushing water I'd heard was a waterfall cascading down the side of the mountain. Lucas let go of my hand. I was stunned to realize that I suddenly felt bereft. I almost reached for his hand. Not because I was afraid, but because I didn't want to break the connection between us.

"Wow, this is awesome." For a minute I forgot that we were being hunted by Evil Scientist and his crew. "I didn't know anything remotely like this existed around here."

"We have a lot of similar places in this forest."

"'We'? You say that like you own the forest."

"Technically it's federal land, but yeah, it's ours."

"What? So there's really a village hidden away out here, like Mason said? Are there really others like you?"

He got eerily still, as though he was trying to decide how much he could trust me. I guess my attitude about not wanting to be whatever he was caused doubts about my sincerity. If I was going to reconnect with Mason's group, I figured the less I knew the better.

"Go ahead and turn on your flashlight," he said, totally ignoring my question. "You'll probably need it where we're going."

"And where is that?"

"Into the waterfall."

THIRTEEN

The waterfall cascaded into a pool. Lucas told me there were some underground streams that fed into a river farther down. Of course, there was also a river high above that furnished the water for the waterfall. I thought maybe we would see it the next day.

But for now, Lucas was holding my hand again and leading me around the edge of the rippling pool. The grass eventually gave way to rocks, pebbles, and small stones that were as slippery as glass. I lost my footing. If Lucas hadn't been holding my hand, I would have tumbled into the pool. Instead, with a tug of my arm, I was tumbling into him, against his warm skin. The shock of it should have had me pulling back, but I found myself melting into him. He felt so good, his skin smooth, his muscles firm.

His arm came around me, holding me in the shelter of his embrace.

As we got closer to the waterfall, it was like walking toward thunder. The rushing water echoed around us and blocked out any other sound. It was disorienting and almost frightening. In contrast, a delicate mist tickled my face. But I knew it was an illusion. Getting caught in that waterfall could kill a person.

Lucas pulled me behind it. I had only a second to run my flashlight over the curtain of rushing water before Lucas drew me into the black abyss.

He released his hold. I shored up my courage and didn't release an embarrassing screech begging him not to leave me. It was quieter in here, the waterfall muted but still present. I swept the beam of the flashlight around the cavern. Someone had been here before us.

"This is one of our lairs," Lucas explained as he crouched to switch on a battery-operated lantern. It provided more light than my flashlight did, so I turned mine off to preserve the batteries. I planned to keep it with me. I felt safe with it. Maybe because my adoptive dad had given it to me. It was like having him here with me. Suddenly I desperately wished he were my real dad. Then all of this might not be real. What was I thinking? It wasn't real anyway.

If it was genetic, then I had to have inherited it from my parents. And they certainly weren't wolves. They didn't heal the way Lucas did when Mason shot him. They died.

"Hungry?" Lucas asked, bringing me out of my morose musings.

"No. Thirsty, though."

He tossed me a bottle of water. The cave was cool. So was the water. Clear plastic crates containing provisions were stacked along the walls. Lucas grabbed a granola bar and started chomping away while he opened another crate and took out a blanket. He walked over to me and draped it around my shoulders.

"You need it more than I do," I said. "At least I'm wearing a shirt."

"There's more. Besides, I can always go furry." He gave me an incredibly sexy grin, and my whole body reacted with a jerk of awareness.

As though suddenly embarrassed, he turned away and walked back to the crate. He took out more blankets and a couple of sleeping bags. He unzipped the bag and laid it down fully opened and spread out. "Thought we could lay down together, share our bodies' heat," he said, indicating that I should stretch out on the bed he'd made. He was still holding the one sleeping bag. I figured he was going to cover us with it.

I'd never slept with a guy before—and even if all we did was sleep, we were still going to be in bed together, our bodies touching, maybe curling into each other. I didn't know if I was ready for the intimacy. On the other hand, absorbing his warmth in this cool cavern sounded heavenly. But sleeping together, even innocently, seemed too soon.

"Uh, after everything that's happened, how can you even think about sleeping?" I asked.

"Honestly, I'm about to collapse."

I'd somehow shoved to the back of my mind that he'd gone through an ordeal. Been shot, no less. Or maybe it was just that he was so good at covering up what he was feeling. Or maybe he *was* superwolf. But I'd been leaning on him since his escape, when maybe I should have been letting him lean on me.

"What do you need me to do to help you?" I asked.

"Just sleep."

I looked at the makeshift bed again.

"I'm not going to attack you the way Mason did," Lucas said.

I glanced over at him. "I know. The thing is—I've never slept with a guy before."

A corner of his mouth hitched up. "It's easy. You close your eyes and dream."

And I could imagine all the things I'd dream lying so close to Lucas. Still, I nodded and stretched out on the sleeping bag. Lucas eased down beside me. Cautiously. I didn't know if it was because he was so exhausted or he thought I might bolt. Or maybe he sensed how stiff and still I was. I'd spent a lot of time thinking about what it would be like the first time I slept with a guy. I hadn't expected it to be in a cave with a guy as dark and dangerous as Lucas. Even though I knew he wouldn't hurt me, for some reason tonight my body didn't feel as though it belonged to me. It wanted to roll over and snuggle up against him.

"Are you okay with the dark or do you want the light left on?" he asked.

"The dark is fine." It wasn't, but no way was I going to admit I was scared of what I was feeling toward him. It seemed like the dark would only intensify it.

I heard the click and the light went out. My eyes quickly adjusted and I could see the waterfall. The moonlight made it look like falling glass. It was somehow very comforting. I slowly began to relax.

"This is my favorite of all the lairs," Lucas said quietly.

I wondered if he'd lied about being able to read my thoughts only when he was in wolf form. Maybe he could read them anytime.

"Looks as though you set this place up like you were

expecting trouble," I said.

"We always expect trouble."

He scooted a little closer. I could feel tiny tremors going through him. "You're cold." I didn't mean for my voice to sound accusing, but it did.

"No, just the aftershocks of an adrenaline rush and a shifting. Warmth helps."

He'd risked everything to save me from Mason. How could I not risk my emotions by moving closer to him?

I rolled over until I was sprawled partway over him. I knew all about adrenaline rushes. When my parents were killed, I'd thought I'd never stop shaking. His arm came around me, holding me close, and I snuggled even closer with my head nestled in the nook of his shoulder. He brought the other sleeping bag over us. We were warm and cozy in our little cocoon. Being next to him like this was wonderful. My body grew limpid. I could smell the heat of his skin, feel the heat of it beneath my cheek and fingers.

"Is it a rush?" I asked quietly, not wanting to disturb the peace settling over us, but wanting to deepen the connection. "Being a wolf, I mean."

"It's not something I think about. It's what I am."

"How did it happen? I mean I know you said it was genetic, but how? Was the first one bitten by a wolf or something?"

His deep laughter rumbled through the cavern. "It's

so stupid when they do that in movies. Why would anyone think getting bitten by anything would turn you into that thing? Same with vampires. So stupid. But no. Lycanthropy isn't something that started because of a bite."

"Then how?"

"We've been here since the dawn of time. But self-preservation made us secretive. Centuries ago, we lived in the general population, but there's always an awareness when we meet our own kind. You've probably felt it when you've met people, but because you didn't know we existed, you might not have recognized it for what it was: like calling to like."

I thought about the first time I met Lindsey last summer. It was as though we were instantly best friends. I'd felt a connection, a history. I'd been able to tell her anything. "Is Lindsey . . . ?" I couldn't say it. It was too incredible.

"Yes," he said quietly. "She hasn't had her transformation. She'll turn seventeen next month."

"We're friends. Why didn't she say something?"

"Would you have believed her? If she couldn't show you?"

"I don't know. I'm not sure I believe you—I believe that you can transform, okay. That *I'm* going to—I'm not convinced. But you're saying there are others like

187

you living out among people?"

"Sure. At schools, universities. We live in communities. We're doctors, lawyers, cops. We're like everyone else, except we shift."

"*Excuse me*, but that makes you *not* like everyone else."

"Okay, you have a point. And yes, there is some risk to us living among the Statics, but it's easier for us to fit in than to have our own country or something. Yes, sometimes we're outed. Our kind has been burned at the stake as witches, hunted down as demons. So centuries ago, the elders created a brotherhood of . . . I guess you can think of them as knights. They're young warriors. We call them Dark Guardians. They're charged with protecting other Shifters."

I scoffed. "I don't think much of their protection techniques. Where were they tonight when you needed them?"

He cleared his throat. "Well, the code is—if a Dark Guardian is stupid enough to get discovered, he's on his own. We risk our lives for others. We don't ask others to risk their lives for us."

I pushed myself up until I could see his face. "Wait a minute. Are you telling me you're a Dark Guardian? That you're a knight or whatever?"

"Yes, exactly. My job is to protect you. That's the

reason I sent the others on and I stayed back, to make sure no one hurt you and to be there when the full moon rose."

He was my protector? That explained the way he always watched me. I wasn't ready to face the full moon and all those ramifications. I still had way too many questions about Lucas. "So you can die."

"Sure. Fire. Bullets."

"But I saw you heal."

"Pretty amazing, huh?" His voice held a hint of pride. "I was just lucky that moronic Mason doesn't know that silver is our Achilles' heel. That part of the Hollywood crap is true. For some reason, a wound inflicted with silver doesn't heal like a normal wound. Knife, sword, bullet—if it's made from silver, we're in some deep shit."

I realized that he trusted me with the secrets to destroying them. Maybe it wasn't trust. Maybe it was self-preservation. Silver had suddenly turned from an accessory to the source of my potential demise.

"Is there any way not to become . . ." My mind was screaming *a freak*, but I couldn't say that. Surely he'd take it as a major insult.

"No," he said quietly. His hand curled around my neck and he eased me back to his shoulder, his arm holding me close to his side as though he could prevent me from feeling the blow of that word. "But it'll be okay. Trust me. I know you have a lot of questions, but I'm fading, Kayla. Let me get some sleep and I'll answer everything tomorrow."

"Okay." I heard his breathing go shallow and felt the slow rise and fall of his chest against my cheek.

I watched the waterfall streaming past. I thought about getting up and just walking straight into it. Let it push me beneath the water and hold me there. I didn't want to be a wolf. Maybe Mason thought that it was totally cool and that people would buy recreational drugs for a couple of hours of being furry, but I wouldn't have taken it if it were free.

I hoped Lucas was wrong. That the connection he felt was something else. Maybe his perception was skewed and he had misread me. I couldn't be a Shifter.

And as far as I was concerned, if I was, my life was suddenly going to suck. Big time.

I was crouched at the edge of the cave, listening to the thundering waterfall, studying my nails. I'd crawled out of the bed while Lucas was still asleep. I had a lot to think about. Part of me wanted to start running from him, from all this, and never stop.

Lucas was so quiet that my heart nearly burst through my chest when he dropped down beside me. I was proud of myself for not giving any indication that he'd startled me.

"You're up early. You okay?" he asked.

Was that a serious question? My world, my life, might not be what I thought it was. Of course I wasn't okay. But I managed to do little more than sigh. "Just thinking. I've never had much luck growing long nails. I guess that's about to change."

He chuckled. Or at least I thought he did. With the waterfall, we had to talk loud, so low chuckles were difficult to hear, but he was smiling. Then, as though he thought we were at risk of ruining our throats if we kept trying to have a conversation where we were, he jerked his head to the side. I followed him back into the cavern.

"Do you know if my adoptive parents know . . . about me, I mean? What I am? Or what I'm going to be?"

"I don't think so. When your parents were killed, you were whisked away before a Dark Guardian could be sent for. Once the government gets involved, it's a little hard to reclaim our own." He opened a crate and tossed me a can of V8.

"I thought wolves were carnivores," I said dryly as I popped the top.

"Wolves are. Shifters aren't." His tone said that I'd insulted him. He handed me a protein bar. "Need to eat. Keep up your strength."

I tore open the wrapper and eyed him dubiously. "You don't think of yourself as a wolf."

"I'm not a wolf. It's a shape I shift into, that's all."

"That's all? Most people don't go all furry and snarling. Not to mention the loonies who are trying to capture you for research."

"What you—what they—see as unusual is normal for me. I've always known it was in my DNA. I couldn't wait until I turned eighteen."

I felt a little hitch in my heart. "I thought you said seventeen."

"Seventeen for girls. Eighteen for guys. Has to do with that whole girls-mature-sooner-than-guys thing."

"Oh, I thought maybe I was going to have a reprieve." The protein bar tasted like sawdust in my mouth.

He opened a snack-sized bag of Double Stuf Oreos and handed me a cookie. Tears sprung to my eyes. I loved these. I looked up at him. He was watching me intently.

"I guess you read my mind about these, too. Will I be able to do that? Read minds?"

"Yeah, but at first it's just confusing babble. You have to learn to sort the voices coming in."

"Is there a werewolf school or something where I can learn all this?"

"We prefer not to use the term *werewolf*. That has

such negative vibes. Name one movie where the werewolf is the good guy. We're Shifters. And no, we don't have a school, but we do have training. It takes place in these woods."

I finished my cookies, drew my knees up to my chest, and wrapped my arms around them. "Does it hurt?"

He knew what I was asking about, and it wasn't the training. He knelt in front of me. He was still barefoot and shirtless. Didn't any of the boxes contain clothes? I wanted so badly to just reach out and run my fingers across his chest and over his shoulders. Instead I focused on his silvery gaze.

"Not if you trust me," he said quietly.

I released a brittle laugh. "Are you sure you're not wrong about me?"

Abruptly he stood up and held out his hand. "Come on. I want to check the perimeter. Then we can relax and enjoy the beautiful day. After all, we're not vampires."

Lucas found a T-shirt. It either wasn't his or it had been his before he'd developed muscles, because it fit him like he'd melted his body into it. I was really beginning to suspect he was reading my mind even when he wasn't in wolf form.

I followed him as he went a short distance into the woods that circled our refuge. He was so graceful—like a Cirque du Soleil performer who is all muscle but moves with powerful grace over the stage. I'd always noticed how buff he was, but now I could see the predator in his movements.

I didn't think they were going to take him by surprise again. And if they did catch up with us, I suspected he'd go after them with a vengeance. Like a Hollywood werewolf. He might not like the way his kind were portrayed on film, but I sensed in him a determination to defend me. It was almost frightening—but it was also thrilling.

Would he be willing to die for me? Did I want him to be willing?

Of course not. But it was still a turn-on to know he took protecting me so seriously. I wasn't quite sure how I felt about the "mate" angle yet. I couldn't deny that I'd been drawn to him from the beginning—with a fierceness that had been so scary, I'd shoved the attraction away and focused on Mason. What I'd felt for Mason, I could deal with. What I felt for Lucas was out of control.

It was even scarier to think maybe Lucas was thinking the same thing about me—but he was strong enough to control it.

As we walked he would suddenly become very still to listen and to sniff the air. It was a rush to think that soon my senses would be heightened—if I truly was a Shifter.

It just seemed impossible.

I probably should have been paying attention to how he was checking things out. I should have been trying to learn whatever it was I was supposed to learn. Instead I was thinking about clothes. Shifting into a wolf was going to be hell on my wardrobe. And what was I supposed to do? Have hidden stashes of clothes all over the place?

"Yes," he said quietly, then stiffened.

But he didn't go as rigid as I did.

"You can read my thoughts even when you're not in wolf form," I accused.

He plowed his strong fingers through his gorgeous hair. "Only when I'm concentrating on you."

"And you're concentrating on me now?"

"How can I not? You smell so good—"

"Are you kidding me? I'm filthy."

"But beneath that is the natural fragrance of your skin. That's what I smell." He started striding back toward the clearing. "Come on. Let's take a swim."

I nearly tripped trying to keep up with him. I was still somewhat in shock over the fact that he was so aware of me, was smelling my skin. "So what? You've got bathing suits stashed in boxes somewhere in that cave?"

He glanced over his shoulder and gave me an utterly

wicked grin. "Who needs bathing suits? Haven't you ever heard of skinny-dipping?"

Okay, there was a chance that tomorrow night he was going to see me in the flesh before he saw me in fur, but I still made him turn his back while I stripped out of my clothes and dove into the pool. It was cool, refreshing, and amazingly clear. When I broke through to the surface, he was already in the water, several feet away. So maybe he was a little bashful, too, about being naked in front of me. Even though I'd already seen his backside.

Treading water, I asked, "So that tattoo on your shoulder. What's it mean?"

"Every male gets a tattoo when he's ready to declare the girl he has chosen to be his mate. It represents her name, written in the ancient language of our pack."

"Who did you choose?"

He gave me a look that asked if I was really that dense.

"Oh." I swallowed hard. I was totally amazed that he could feel something that strongly and not let on. How could he declare his feelings to a tattoo artist without knowing if I returned them? "I didn't even think you noticed me last summer."

"Oh, I noticed. It was like *bam*, right to the gut."

"You didn't say anything."

"You'd just turned sixteen and were still in high school, and I was going off to college."

"I'm still in high school and you're still in college."

"But you're older. And it's just a year until you're finished with high school. Once you graduate, you could go to the same university I do."

"So I'll see my adopted parents again?"

"Sure. You'll return home at the end of summer—a little different than you were when you arrived here."

That's an understatement. Even if I didn't shift, I was never going to forget everything I'd learned—and I'd be looking everywhere for Shifters.

"We live out in the world, among the Statics," he continued. "Pretty normal. Or as normal as we can be when we're charged with guarding the secret of our existence."

I was still dumbstruck by what he'd decided last summer when he met me. "But the decisions you made last summer about us—what if you never saw me again?"

"I knew where you lived, Kayla. I would have come for you, if Lindsey hadn't convinced you to join us here this summer. I wouldn't have let you discover the truth about yourself alone."

"So Lindsey knew what you felt."

"Yeah, but there's a code. You don't tell someone who a guy has chosen."

I was flattered—and unnerved.

As though he was a typical guy who wasn't comfortable discussing his feelings, he began to swim across the pool. Long, powerful strokes. The muscles in his back bunching and flexing. The tattoo—my name in ancient letters—seemed to pulse.

He'd made a commitment to me without knowing if I'd ever reciprocate. I was immensely flattered, but I also felt incredibly overwhelmed. The depths of what he felt for me went beyond anything I'd ever felt for a guy. And yet, I couldn't deny there was something between us.

I started to backstroke in the opposite direction, realized I was flashing a little more than I wanted to, and went back to dog-paddling. Or in my case, I suppose it was actually wolf-paddling.

He came back toward me and stopped about two feet away.

"Your tattoo. Rafe has one similar to it."

"Yeah."

My eyes widened. "He's a were—" I stopped myself in the nick of time. "He's a Shifter?"

"Yes."

"Whose name is on his back?"

"I can't tell you. I took an oath of secrecy."

Well, that was irritating. It wasn't that I was a gossip,

but I was very curious.

"What if you guess wrong?" I asked. "What if you misread the feeling? What if the girl doesn't feel for you what you feel for her?" I had so many questions. I didn't really understand how this mate thing worked, but it seemed bigger than either of us.

"It's a bummer. You go through life with some chick's name on your shoulder, and no other girl is going to want you because you gave your devotion to someone else first."

"That's harsh."

"It ensures we don't choose lightly."

It was really overwhelming to think he'd selected me—or destiny had. I wasn't quite sure how this whole fate/mate thing worked. "But you barely knew me last summer."

"I knew enough, Kayla. For us, when you meet your soul mate . . . you just *know*. I don't know how to explain it. Didn't you feel anything when you met me?"

"Scared," I admitted. "Overwhelmed. I definitely noticed you, but I never thought about you and me. I mean, look at you! You're older, hot, in shape . . . and I'm all crazy red hair and freckles."

He grinned. "I like your red hair and freckles. And I like that you have an inner strength that I don't think you recognize. You took a big risk freeing me from that cage."

"What they did was wrong."

"But not everyone would have done anything about it. And when you were beating down on Mason—I loved it."

I felt the heat of embarrassment warm my face. "I can't believe I fell for all his smooth talking."

"He fooled a lot of people."

"Not you."

"I had some suspicions, but that's all they were. I come from a society that for centuries has been persecuted based on witch hunts. I don't make accusations without proof."

Even if waiting for that proof had nearly cost him his freedom, maybe even his life.

"What about Connor? And Brittany? Are they—" My mind was suddenly reeling.

"Most sherpas are. It's how we control what part of the wilderness Statics are allowed to see. If we kept them out completely, they'd get suspicious. As it is, we guide them where we want them to go and keep them away from where we don't want them to be."

"Mason believes there's a village somewhere out here."

His face went all hard, his eyes like smoothly polished stones. "Yeah. I'm still trying to figure out how he got tipped off to that. I mean, there are legends, but he seemed to be just a little too sure."

In my surprise, I forgot to keep treading water. I went under, closing my mouth just in time to avoid having to resurface sputtering. I really do like to limit just how foolish I look. I pushed myself back up.

Now Lucas had a quizzical look on his face that reminded me of a dog tilting its head in confusion. I would have laughed if I weren't still absorbing what he'd said. "There's really a village?"

"Wolford. The elders live there. The rest of us meet up there for the summer solstice. It's pretty well hidden. No way will kooky Keane and his robotic followers find it."

I wasn't so sure, but I was thinking of something else he'd said. "Why are you trying to figure out how they got tipped off? You like puzzles? You're the strategist?"

"I thought you figured it out. I'm the pack leader. The alpha male of the group."

I didn't know why I didn't realize it before. The way Rafe deferred to him. I'd always thought Lucas was just the one in charge of the sherpas.

"So how does that work? Do the *elders* you mentioned vote on it?"

"No. You fight for it. While in wolf form. You challenge and take out the current leader."

Like wild animals? What was he? Man or beast?

"And that's what you did? Just beat him up?"

He held my gaze as though he needed to judge my reaction to his words. "It's a fight to the death."

This time when I stopped treading water and went under, I wasn't sure I wanted to surface. There were things about his society that I wasn't sure I wanted to be part of.

FOURTEEN

"Devlin was pack leader before me."

Lucas and I were no longer in the water. We were dressed again and lying on a blanket near the pond but far enough away that the waterfall didn't drown out our words. This place seemed too peaceful for everything I was learning about Lucas. The sky was so incredibly blue, with fluffy white clouds drifting by. When darkness arrived, I'd be that much closer to a full moon. My body tingled with the thought—as though it couldn't wait. But psychologically, I couldn't accept that I was going to go all furry. I'd broken my arm when I was eight. They'd taken X-rays. Surely a Shifter's bones were different, were multijointed. How else could they transform from a human to such a different creature? It was inconceivable to me.

"I didn't get a chance to kill him," Lucas said, and I heard the disappointment in his voice. "He ran off, like a coward. So my ascension to the role of pack leader is a little tainted."

I rolled my head to the side and studied his handsome profile. He was focused on the sky. Maybe telling me all the dark secrets about his past was as hard for him as it was for me. I couldn't imagine killing anyone—but to do it to gain power . . . I wanted to understand Lucas, but his was a scary world.

"Why did you want to be in charge?" I asked.

He turned his head to watch me. "Devlin was an incredibly bad leader. He kept putting the others at risk. Taking chances. Exposing the existence of our society. He had to be stopped. But in the end I didn't stop him. I'm pretty sure the black wolf you saw—it was him."

"So when you said he had a wolf for a pet . . . ?"

"I was twisting the truth. Sometimes we have to do that. Just like the night Keane was talking about were-wolves and we were all making fun of it like it was ludicrous."

I could see where a lot of fast thinking would have to take place in order to not give things away.

"So you think maybe he's how the Keanes found out about you . . . the Shifters?"

He gave me a dark grin. "About you, too. You're one of us."

"Yeah." He was convinced. I wasn't. Bummer for him if he'd chosen a non-Shifter. I sat up and crossed my legs beneath me. "I know I should probably be thrilled about that—"

"It's a lot to wrap your head around," he said as he shoved himself up on an elbow.

"Do I need to do something to prepare?" It seemed like I should do something. Obviously I no longer had a reason to shave my legs. I ran my hand over my bare legs, and tried to make light of what I couldn't really accept. "As a wolf, will my legs be bald if I shave?"

"Was my wolf face bald?"

I released a self-conscious laugh. "No. You actually were as gorgeous as a wolf as you are . . ." I let my voice trail off. Had I really wanted to confess that?

He gave me a crooked grin. "You think I'm cute."

"Cute, no! Definitely not. Beautiful . . . yes."

He pushed up until he was sitting and leaned toward me. "I think you're beautiful, too. I've thought that from the first time I saw you."

I felt myself grow pleasantly warm. "Is that the reason you looked at me all the time?"

"Yeah. I figured you'd see how I felt. Guess it was kinda creepy, though, having this guy watch you and never talk to you."

"You don't seem the shy type."

"The first time I saw you it was like something had slammed into my chest. Seriously. I didn't think I was ever going to breathe right again. I didn't know what to say to you."

He skimmed his fingers along my cheek. Looking at him now, he appeared to be any normal teenage boy.

"The night before the sherpas left, you and Rafe had an argument."

"Yeah. He knew you were one of us, thought I was being irresponsible to leave you behind. But I didn't want to force you to go, to make you resent me, and I hadn't figured out how to tell you yet about our abilities. And okay, to be honest, I was jealous that you were so into Mason."

"I don't know that I was really into him. I liked him because he was uncomplicated, because he didn't make me feel all these insane things that you do. That pull you were talking about—I'd never felt anything like it before. So what is it? Like an animal bond or something?"

"It can be intense, but it can't make you feel what you're not really feeling. If that makes sense. We feel these primal urges because we walk the fine line between man and beast, but at our core we're human. We just have the ability to shift into another form."

"You say that like it's nothing."

"I grew up watching people shifting back and forth with the ease of someone clicking the remote to flip through channels on the TV."

"So who coached you?" I asked.

"Males go through it alone."

"Doesn't that make it more painful?"

"Doesn't seem fair, does it? But it's a form of natural selection. The weaker males don't survive."

"Were you afraid?"

"I couldn't wait, but then I knew what was coming. When I was a kid, my parents took me into the woods, explained things, showed me—"

"Oh my God!" I glanced around quickly because it was safer than looking at him or inside of myself.

He sat up straight. "What? What is it?"

"My parents . . . those deer hunters said they saw wolves." I buried my face in my hands. "What if it was my parents? Showing me? We ran. Mom pushed me back beneath some brush. There was growling." I'd repressed the images. "There *were* wolves," I said with a certainty I'd never before felt.

I lowered my hands and met Lucas's gaze, knowing the

devastation he must have seen in my eyes. "The wolves. Could they have been my parents?"

"It makes sense that they might have been."

Only if I bought into the whole I-am-a-werewolf-too idea. I was having a difficult time accepting that.

"If you die in wolf form, what happens?" I asked.

"Our species always reverts back to human form right before death."

"So the hunters might have been correct when they said they shot wolves?"

Lucas nodded.

I shook my head. "No, my parents weren't naked. And if they were shot, wouldn't they have healed?"

"Not if they were shot in the heart or the head."

"But they would have been naked," I mused. And they weren't. At least I didn't remember them that way.

Last summer I hadn't wanted to go to the part of the forest where they'd died. Suddenly, I realized that in order to face my past and present fears, I needed to return to that place. I didn't even know how to find out where it was.

Later that night I prowled around the cavern with nervous energy I couldn't explain. Or maybe I just didn't want to face the truth of it. Spending the afternoon with Lucas in our isolated world here had made me more aware of him.

I thought I could smell the scent of his skin. It was going to be more difficult to lie with him tonight and just hold him and be held by him.

I walked to the edge of the cavern, closed my eyes, and listened to the water crashing down. I wanted to empty my mind of all thoughts. But one remained: If I didn't shift tomorrow night, would I lose him?

In spite of the roaring waterfall and my closed eyes, I knew the moment he stepped behind me.

"Kayla?"

I loved the deep rumble of his voice and the way my name sounded when he spoke it. I turned to face him.

"Nothing between us has changed," he said.

"Everything's changed. I know you better now. It's like I've had a crash course in Lucas Wilde. I'm feeling things I've never felt before."

"Good things?"

"Scary things. Intense. What if I'm not what you think I am?"

"You mean you're not brave?"

I released a self-conscious laugh and shook my head. "That's not what—"

"You don't have an inner strength? You're not courageous? You're going to change, Kayla, but what I feel for you isn't because you *will* change—it's because of everything that won't change."

209

"Oh." I didn't know what to say to that. I thought it was probably as close to a declaration of love as I might ever get.

"Come on." He took my hand and led me over to the sleeping bag.

I drew comfort while wrapped within Lucas's arms. I could hear his heart pounding, feel the warmth of his body. It was different tonight. Our closeness had changed, evolved. He wasn't Lucas, my boss. He was Lucas, my Dark Guardian.

Even if I didn't think I needed a guardian, I knew he'd always be there.

"Will it happen"—*if it happens*, I thought—"as soon as the moon appears?"

"No, not until the moon reaches its zenith."

"How will I know?"

"You'll start to feel . . . different. Don't let it scare you. I know you haven't known for very long, but for us morphing is a natural part of life—like puberty."

"Yeah, well, I've had a lot of unpleasant cramps during puberty."

He pressed his lips to my forehead. "So now you'll have cramps all over, but they come and they go quickly."

I had a thousand questions as my time drew nearer. "When you're in wolf form, do you think like a wolf?"

"I don't know. I don't know how a wolf thinks."

I released a bubble of laughter, before going quiet. "You know what I'm asking."

"It's still you, Kayla. Inside. You just look a little different. When I'm in wolf form, I'm more aggressive, better able to fight—that's the reason I shifted when the bear was going to attack you. I can run faster as a wolf, so if I need to get somewhere quickly, I'll usually shift."

"I thought you were pretty fast last night—when you weren't in wolf form."

"Most Shifters are fast and strong. Our bodies constantly get a workout." He brushed his lips along my temple. "You're going to do fine, Kayla."

A shiver went through me as his voice rumbled near my ear. His skin was warm against my fingers where they rested on his chest.

"You said I was your mate," I said, my voice low and hesitant. "Does that mean we get married?"

"Not necessarily. Usually mates marry, but not always. We'll go through the whole dating scene if you want to go out with me. But you're not forced to be with me—if it's not what you want."

His voice had grown very quiet.

"If I didn't want to be your mate, would you find another?"

"No, I'd just be alone."

My heart did a little stutter. I rose up on my elbow and looked down on him. The moon—just a little shy of being full—was large and bright, shining through the waterfall as though it were a gossamer curtain. "That's not fair."

"I know. The male Shifters get the raw end of the deal. They feel what they feel, and the females choose."

"Do they ever fight over a female?"

"Sure. Sometimes a girl wants to know who's the strongest, who wants her the most. We're human, but we're also animal."

"I don't know if I'll ever wrap my mind around all this."

He cradled my cheek with his hand and threaded his fingers up into my hair. "Are you freaked out about what I am?"

Strangely, I wasn't freaked out by him. By myself, yes. I was definitely having some problems coping with that, but Lucas was just Lucas. Lying here with him, I could forget that he was sometimes furry.

"No," I answered truthfully.

"Good." He rolled over until I was on my back and he was above me. He cradled my cheek with his large, warm hand. "Good," he repeated.

Then he kissed me. It wasn't like any kiss I'd ever had before, but then, I hadn't expected it to be. It was, after all, Lucas. And he wasn't like any guy I'd ever known before. His lips were soft and gentle, as though he wasn't sure that I would want this. But how could I not?

I'd wished for it on my birthday.

He pulled back and looked at me quizzically. "You smile when you're being kissed?"

I broadened my smile. "My birthday wish just came true. When I blew out the candles, I wished you'd kiss me."

"Really?"

"Strange, I know. I wasn't even sure I liked you. You were always so intense." I reached up and combed my fingers through his hair. "Now I know why."

I wanted to believe what he believed, that I was going to shift, that I was his destiny—but it all seemed too amazing.

He drew me back into the circle of his arms. I pressed a light kiss to his shoulder.

"We should sleep now," he said. "You'll need all your strength tomorrow night."

Practical Lucas. I wanted to get corny and say something like, "Strength? Who needs strength when I've got you?"

But he was right. Tomorrow everything would change. And according to him, that included me.

* * *

"Kayla, wake up."

There was an urgency in Lucas's voice that I hadn't heard before. I'd fallen asleep wrapped in the cocoon of his embrace. I didn't know when he'd left me, but now he was crouched beside me, shaking my shoulder. I squinted at him. I hadn't expected to fall so soundly asleep, and I resented that he was waking me up. "What's wrong?"

"I don't know. It's just a feeling I have."

The words hit me like a jolt of caffeine. And I could feel it, too. It was like that first night, the tingly feeling I'd had, that sense of being watched.

"Mason. They found us," I said.

"No way. They didn't have trackers in their group. And this area is too well hidden."

"We didn't know they had scientists in their group either—and they did."

"Good point." He shoved a backpack into my arms. "Here, you wear it. I may have to shift."

I started pulling on my boots. "What are we going to do?"

"Have a look around and, if we need to, run."

He stood up with that graceful, lithe movement he had. Then he reached down, took my hand, and pulled me to my feet. Still holding my hand, he began leading me toward the waterfall. "I want you to wait by the entrance until I've checked—"

A figure stepped into the entrance, and just like in some corny movie, he was wielding a gun. It wasn't anyone I knew, but Lucas stiffened and shoved me behind him. He eased a little closer to the waterfall, then he tried to push me back. "Go out the other side."

"Oh, Lucas, do you really want her to miss the party? And where are your manners? Shouldn't you introduce your brother to your girlfriend?"

Devlin? This was Devlin? I peered around Lucas for a better look. I thought if it weren't for all the hatred in his eyes, Devlin might have been handsome. At one time he probably was. What had changed him?

Lucas emitted a low growl and went very still.

"Don't even think about morphing," Devlin said. "I loaded a silver bullet into the gun. If I shoot you while you're in wolf form, it's hopeless—you'll be dead. Maybe not immediately, but eventually."

"I know how silver works. What do you want?"

"The return of my rightful place as leader of the pack would be nice."

"The pack leader serves as leader of the Dark Guardians. He protects the existence of our kind. You led Keane to us."

"That's just a guess on your part, but it so happens that you're right."

"Did you lead them here?"

"No. Those idiots. I washed my hands of them when they didn't kill you. They took off in their choppers. I imagine they'll be back. But I don't care. They were supposed to do an autopsy on you, study you. Instead they planned to draw blood and swab your mouth. Where's the fun in that?"

"You've put our entire existence at risk."

Devlin released a deep sigh. I kept trying to find even a hint of Lucas in him, but I couldn't. His hair was only one shade: black. His eyes were a lifeless gray. What had happened to make him the way he was?

"Our existence was already at risk. There are so few of us left. Do you think any Static female is going to mate with us? God, I hate what we are."

"Just because one girl—"

"One girl? She was everything to me. My own family wouldn't accept her. She wouldn't accept me. I shifted to save her life one night when some thugs attacked her in an alley, and all I did was horrify her. Do you know what it is to name your mate and then know you can't have her? To know you're destined to spend your life alone and lonely? To always be empty and have no love to fill the void?"

"I know it was hard—"

"You don't know anything! But you will. Before the

next full moon, you will. You'll know what it is to hate what you are. I went to Keane because I wanted to find a cure for what I am. I wanted him to make me normal. Instead he wanted to make everyone like us."

"So you're not working with them?" I asked.

I felt Lucas stiffen again. I knew he wanted me to quietly disappear, but his brother was dangerous.

Devlin didn't answer my question. Instead he said, "If you're not with her when she shifts for the first time, you could lose her completely. Your heart will break and then you'll understand my pain."

"I'm going to be there for her."

"We'll see." Devlin began moving slowly into the cave. Lucas turned to face him, pushing me away in the process.

I don't know what I was expecting. Maybe I thought they both would shift and go at it. I mean, if Devlin wanted Lucas to suffer, he needed him alive.

So the explosion echoing through the cavern and Lucas flying backward into the waterfall stunned me, and my instincts took over.

My horrified scream was lost in the roar of the rushing water as I dove in after him.

Being a strong swimmer was an advantage when tons of water was crushing down on you. Those rescue lessons I'd taken when I'd worked as a lifeguard didn't hurt either.

Any other time I might have marveled at how luminescent the pool was with the moon shining through the clear water, but all my efforts were focused on retrieving Lucas. I wrapped an arm beneath his arm and around his chest before shooting back to the surface. I swam to the edge of the pool, away from the waterfall.

"Help me, Lucas," I ordered.

I heard him groan, felt him trembling, and was aware of his warm blood flowing around me. I tried to push him out of the water. "Lucas, please."

With another groan and herculean effort, he surged up and belly flopped onto the grass. I shoved him completely out of the water. Then I hauled myself out and knelt beside him.

"How bad is it?" I asked.

"Bad," he answered through clenched teeth.

I eased up his T-shirt. With the moonlight and the faint rays of the approaching dawn, I could see the dark ragged hole in his side and the blood flowing from it. I tore off my shirt, leaving just my tank underneath it. I'd tear it off, too, if I had to. I pressed my shirt to his side to try to staunch the river of blood.

"Are you sure you can't shift?" I asked. "Just for a few seconds?"

"If he does, he'll die."

I was startled by Devlin's voice. I wasn't sure when he'd joined us, but I should have known he'd want to see his handiwork.

"He can feel the burning of the silver. He knows I wasn't lying about the bullet," Devlin said with satisfaction in his voice. "I don't want him dead. I just wanted to prevent him from stopping me."

"Stopping you from what?"

He jerked me to my feet and before I could protest, he'd looped and lassoed a rope around my wrists, securing them tightly, then jerking me toward him. "From taking you away."

He started pulling me and I dug in my heels. "You're insane."

"According to Nietzsche, 'There is always some madness in love.'" He glanced over at me and smiled a cruel smile. "I was a philosophy major."

"Lucas did what he did to protect the pack. You can't punish him for that."

"Of course I can. What I'm doing only has to make sense to me. That's the beauty of madness. Now, you don't want to fight me, because I have more bullets in this gun. Killing you would take you away from him permanently."

"I'm going to die anyway. Lucas said I wouldn't survive if he wasn't with me."

"Guess we'll find out."

He tugged on the rope, pulling me along behind him. I wasn't afraid of dying. Okay, I was. I was terrified by the thought. I didn't want to leave Lucas behind, but I didn't have a choice. I didn't go easily, but neither did I resist with everything in me.

I glanced back over my shoulder. Lucas was struggling to his knees. *Please don't follow,* I thought. *Save yourself. Wait for me.*

I was optimistic that one way or another I could escape and find help for Lucas.

It was a hard climb up the side of the forested slope that created the basin around the waterfall and pond—especially as my hands were bound. Lucas and I had come in at the bottom of the slope. Devlin wanted to leave from the top.

I was exhausted when we finally reached our destination. The sky was awash in a reddish orange to herald the new day. From up here, I could see the river that created the powerful waterfall. I had no time or desire to appreciate its magnificence.

Breathing heavily, I dropped to my knees. "Give me a minute to rest, please."

"I forget how little stamina humans have before the first shift." He was still holding the rope attached to my hands. I wondered if I tugged on it could I jerk him over the edge of the cliff and back into the valley that we'd crawled out of.

"Lucas is your brother," I pointed out, panting.

"Your point?"

"How can you do this to him?"

He crouched in front of me. "He challenged me! He took my place as leader. Okay, so maybe I was dancing at the edge of responsibility—but I'd lost Jenny. They could have cut me some slack."

"Mason told me that his college roommate—"

"Yeah, that was me. He was such a geeky kid, in awe of his father. When he started talking about Bio-Chrome, I thought it was destiny."

"If you wanted a cure so badly, why not let them experiment on *you*?"

"Because I didn't trust Keane not to portray me for what I am: a freak." He shrugged. "Besides, I was in the mood for a little revenge." He stood up and jerked me to my feet. "Now let's go."

I heard a low, threatening growl. There were probably a hundred wolves in this forest, and I had no idea how many Shifters. But I knew before I turned around and saw the familiar multicolored coat of fur that it was Lucas in wolf form. He bared his sharp incisors.

"Dammit, Lucas, what did you do—dig the bullet out? You are determined to prove yourself, aren't you?

Unfortunately I don't have any more silver bullets. Do you know how expensive they are?" Devlin shoved me to the ground. I hit with a jarring thud. "So I guess we'll settle this in the way of our kind."

From my position, I could see Lucas's side. He was still bleeding. Even with the bullet gone, I guessed he couldn't heal completely. He'd be weaker—

A shirt flew at me and landed over my face. By the time I could snatch it off, Devlin had shifted and a black wolf was crouched near me. The black wolf I'd seen the night of the beer party. He was larger than Lucas. His teeth seemed longer, sharper.

Mason had mumbled something about the eyes not changing. I understood what he meant now. Shifters retained their human eyes. I could see Lucas in the silver and the madness that was Devlin in the gray.

I knew this would be a fight to the death, as it was supposed to have been when Lucas first challenged Devlin's place as pack leader. I knew Lucas was weak and wounded. I knew Devlin was strong and insane—and there was a certain strength that came with madness. Lucas was risking the loss of everything. Devlin had already lost it all. He risked nothing, and that made him the more dangerous of the two.

I knew that Devlin had every advantage. That I was likely to lose Lucas, lose what I'd only just discovered.

I love you.

The words were just a whisper in my mind. But it was enough. Lucas heard them. His head jerked toward me.

It was a tactical mistake. As Devlin launched himself at Lucas, I realized that with my words, I'd sentenced Lucas to death.

FIFTEEN

With a challenging growl, Lucas catapulted himself toward Devlin.

Teeth bared, the brothers collided in midair, snarling. Their strong jaws were snapping, and their claws were tearing through fur to reach vulnerable flesh. I could smell the earthy scent of fresh blood on the air, and my nostrils flared in response. Was it because I was that much closer to a full moon and would soon be what they'd become?

They slammed to the ground, scrambling apart to regroup. They slowly circled, each searching for a weakness—a vulnerability—in the other. Lucas waited, and I knew he was hoarding what little strength he had left. Devlin lunged.

Lucas sprung to the side. Devlin landed. Lucas pounced onto his back, biting into Devlin's shoulder. Devlin yelped from pain and maybe surprise, too. Surely he hadn't expected Lucas to be so aggressive. Devlin bucked, trying to throw Lucas off. Lucas bit Devlin again.

They rolled. They snapped at each other. They broke apart and came back together. Over and over. I could see Lucas's strength waning. I kept my eyes on him, wondering what I could do to help and knowing with a sense of helplessness that there was nothing. Tomorrow it might have been a different story; tomorrow I might have been more help, with my first shift behind me. But for now, Lucas had to battle alone.

I knew Devlin would show no mercy. Devlin would go for his throat if the opportunity presented itself.

They fought on. Tumbling, one over the other, they were getting closer and closer to the edge of the cliff. They broke apart as though they realized that was the only way to slow their momentum. I tried to blank my mind. I didn't want Lucas to know how frightened I was for him. I didn't want to make my previous mistake of distracting him. His breathing was labored, his side coated in blood.

I clutched Devlin's shirt only because it was something

to hold on to. I glanced over at his discarded pants and saw the gun. I scrambled over to it and lifted it. It was hard to hold with my hands tied, but I managed. My adoptive dad had taken me to the shooting range lots of times. I was pretty good with a gun, if I did say so myself. Even though up until this point, all my targets had been outlines on paper.

I aimed it, but Lucas was in the way. Was this his battle and his battle alone to fight? Would he hate me for killing his brother? The bullet wasn't silver. The odds were it wouldn't kill him, but it might give Lucas a chance. I moved over to the side, hoping for a better angle.

Devlin launched himself. Lucas sprung up and slammed into Devlin, sending them both careening over the edge of the cliff.

My scream followed them down.

Still holding the gun uselessly, I rushed to the edge of the cliff and looked over it. I could see Devlin, partway down, impaled by the broken branch of a tree. He wasn't moving and he was in human form. I assumed he was dead.

My heart was thudding painfully in my chest. Where was Lucas?

Then I saw him, still in wolf form, making his way painfully back up the side of the cliff.

"No!" I yelled. "Go back down. I'll meet you at the bottom."

But he kept trudging upward until he reached level ground. He trotted over to me. He licked my chin. I wrapped my arms around him, buried my face in his fur, and wept.

After all that, my mind was blank. I didn't know what to think, except that maybe he'd welcome the silence.

When my embarrassing breakdown was finished, I leaned back and looked into his silver eyes that remained the same whether he was wolf or human. "I was so scared. I know he was your brother and you didn't want to fight him, but he forced you. It's not your fault he's dead."

He threw back his head and howled. It was the most lonesome sound I'd ever heard. When the echo of his sorrow and pain fell into silence he collapsed against me.

I didn't know what to do, but I knew if I couldn't stop the bleeding in his side, he was going to die.

His howl had been more than a reflection of his suffering. It had been a call to the others. Within an hour, a dozen wolves had reached us. A black wolf with brown eyes cautiously approached.

Using Devlin's shirt, I'd been able to stop the bleeding, but Lucas was too heavy for me to carry anywhere and too exhausted to move himself.

Lucas lifted his head slightly and I knew he was communicating with the wolf. I also suspected who it was: Rafe, who'd always been Lucas's second-in-command when we were taking the Keanes into the wilderness. He disappeared down the cliff and into the cavern for several minutes and when he returned, he was in human form and wearing clothes. He took charge.

The other wolves didn't seem inclined to reveal their true identities, but when it became apparent that Rafe couldn't get Lucas into the lair behind the waterfall alone, another wolf stepped forward. His fur was an almost golden hue, his eyes blue. Connor, I realized. He, too, went behind the waterfall and returned clothed and in human form.

Once we had Lucas back in the cavern and beneath blankets, he shifted. I wouldn't have expected Shifters to be so modest. Maybe it was only because I wasn't one of them yet.

Rafe examined his wound. "Looks like it's healing slowly."

"Yeah, if I go back into wolf form for a few hours, I think it'll heal enough not to be bothersome."

"So why did you shift?" I asked, squeezing his hand.

He gave me a tired smile. "Because I wanted to talk with you, be there for you." He touched my cheek. "I know what you're thinking, but you don't know what

I'm thinking—not yet anyway."

I wished Rafe and Connor would leave so I could curl up against Lucas. I just wanted to be alone with him.

Rafe said, "I'm going to pack some gauze around the wound to slow the bleeding." He gave Lucas a pointed stare. "You should have called for us as soon as you started running into trouble. You don't have to face all our problems by yourself."

"Think you could chew him out later?" I asked. "He's really been through enough today."

"Do you want Devlin taken back to the village?" Connor asked.

Lucas nodded. "Yeah, my parents need to know."

"We'll see to him," Rafe said. He and Connor left.

I touched his side near the wound. "I can't believe you dug the bullet out."

"It wasn't that bad. He didn't hit anything vital. I'm surprised it didn't go through on its own."

"So it'll heal now?"

"It'll take most of the day, and it hurts like a bitch, but I should be okay by tonight."

By the time I was supposed to transform.

"We should both sleep," he said. "It's been a rough day and tonight's going to be challenging."

"Okay." I started to move back a little, and then changed my mind. I leaned forward and kissed him slowly. Whether I changed tonight or not, I was falling for Lucas . . . hard.

I drew away and gave him a soft smile. I twisted around and removed my boots. When I turned back, he was a wolf.

I nestled up against his side. Sleep seemed impossible when I knew what awaited me tonight. So I was surprised when darkness claimed me quickly.

SIXTEEN

When I woke up, it was early nightfall. Lucas was still sleeping when I crept out of the cavern and eased out from behind the waterfall. It was one of those weird nights where the moon was visible at the same time that the sun was. I'd always found the moon peaceful, but not tonight. Tonight it seemed ominous, a sign of change that I wasn't sure I wanted to face.

I glanced around. No sign existed of the wolves who'd been here earlier, but I had a feeling they were still around, guarding us. They knew what was supposed to happen tonight. It seemed to me that I should feel different. Instead I wondered what my senior year of high school was going to be like if I had a boyfriend at a university in another state. I was concerned with clothes and shoes and grades. Typical teenage stuff. I just didn't know if I'd be typical anymore.

I felt Lucas's presence before I heard him or saw him. He came to stand beside me. He'd shifted back to human form. Even though he was still recovering from his wound, I felt strength emanating from him.

"The others are still here, aren't they?" I asked.

"Yes. Devlin said the Keanes had left. Tonight wouldn't be a good night for them to return. The first shift goes much easier if there are no interruptions, if we're not distracted by other things."

I glanced at his side. He was wearing a T-shirt and I couldn't see his bandages, but I knew they were there. "How are you feeling?"

"Not bad for someone who got shot. I've gotten so used to shifting to heal wounds that I'm a little impatient that it hasn't healed completely, but I'm going to be all right."

"He could have killed you."

"But he didn't. And now it's your survival we have to focus on."

My mouth went dry. I was almost as scared right now as I'd been this afternoon. "If you're right about what's going to happen, I guess after tonight I won't be just a girl anymore."

He gave me a sad smile. "You never were, Kayla."

I nodded. "I know this probably sounds totally insane—and I know it's not like we're getting married—but I really feel grungy. I'd love to pretty myself up."

"A lot of the guys bring the girls here for their first transformation. There's a box over there with a lot of girl stuff in it. I'll show you. Then I have some things to prepare, too."

I found everything I needed in the cavern. I guessed that they were used to girls feeling like they had to be at their best when going through their first shift. There were little samples of everything, like you find in a hotel. Using the very edge of the waterfall where the water wasn't so harsh, I shampooed and showered. I applied a lotion to my skin. I combed out my hair and finger-fluffed it until it dried. I left it loose, hanging past my shoulders. I had a brief moment of wondering what my fur would look like before shutting down the thought. I didn't really want to contemplate the enormity of what was going to happen in a few hours.

I bundled up my clothes, then dropped them near our sleeping bags. Arranged over some containers was a wrap that Lucas suggested I wear. It would provide me with cover without hampering my movements until I shifted. Then it would just fall away.

It was white and silky and seemed appropriate for a first-time Shifter. I draped it around my shoulders. It had enough volume and folds that I didn't have to clutch the opening to keep it closed. I guessed after thousands of years the Shifters had figured out what they needed for this moment.

I walked back to the waterfall and stared at the rush of water. I didn't have Lucas's certainty that I was going to change. While I was afraid of what the transformation might be like, I was more terrified that if it didn't occur, in spite of his reassurances, I'd lose Lucas.

Lucas and I ate by moonlight. We sat on a black cape, similar to my white one. I assumed it was his and wondered why he wasn't already wearing it. Apparently there were rituals involved here that I didn't yet know about.

Dinner was simple: just prepackaged sandwiches and protein bars. Lucas told me to eat plenty because I'd need my strength. Sipping my bottled water, I watched as the moon rose higher.

"So after the first shift, I can change at will?" I asked, wanting to know as much as possible in case it did happen.

Lucas was stuffing our trash into the front pocket of the backpack. He was all about not littering our environment. He glanced up at me. "Yeah."

"So, how do I do that?"

"The first shift, you have no control over. Your body is going to do what it needs to do to teach itself to shift.

When you're ready to shift back to human form, just close your eyes and envision yourself as a human. Your body will take over."

"What if it doesn't? What if I get stuck?"

He grinned. "I've never heard of anyone getting stuck in one form. If you think you're in trouble, just let me know." He shifted away as though suddenly uncomfortable. "Just remember that I'll be able to read all your thoughts . . . and you'll be able to read mine."

"That's how we'll communicate?"

"Yeah."

"This is going to be so freaking weird. Are you sure you don't have me confused with someone else?"

"I'm sure."

"So what time will all this happen? When will the moon be at its zenith?"

"Sometime around midnight."

I nodded. "And what do you do?"

"If you accept me—"

"Wait, what do you mean if I accept you?"

"You have to accept me as your mate."

"How do I do that?"

He grinned again. "With a kiss."

I smiled back at him, then my nerves kicked in and I grew serious. "So this is a shifting and a mating ritual?"

I thought he was blushing again. "It doesn't go any

further than a kiss . . . unless both parties want it to."

"Have you ever done it? I mean, as a wolf?"

He laughed. It was a deep rich sound, the first time I'd ever heard him truly laugh. It made me feel good, made some of the tension inside me uncoil.

"I can't believe you asked me that," he said.

"What? You never even thought about it?"

He gave me a wry grin. "No, I've never done it as a wolf."

"How about . . . you know. In human form."

He took my hand and shook his head. "Wolves mate for life."

I swallowed hard. "So you've been, like, waiting for me?"

"My whole life."

No wonder Devlin had lost it. But I didn't want to think about him or all the heavy stuff that Lucas might be dealing with. I needed to get through tonight so I could help him get through the baggage he'd picked up. My therapist was going to have a field day analyzing me when I got back from summer vacation.

"So this silky thing we're sitting on, you'll wear it?"

He nodded.

"And you stay in human form until . . .?"

"We shift together—or as close together as possible."

"And you tell me what to do?"

He nodded again.

I squeezed his hands. "Look, I know this is coming, but . . . I can't just sit here and wait for it. Don't take this wrong, but I need to walk around. And I need to be alone for a while to psych myself up."

"Okay."

"Okay." I should have felt relief that he didn't argue. He needed to rest anyway. It was still a couple hours until the time for my transformation. I got up and started walking along the edge of the clearing.

What amazed me was that it was such a calm night. It felt like there should be storms, thunder, and lightning. Like the world should feel the turmoil that was rumbling inside me. This morning I'd thought the impassioned words *I love you* when Lucas had faced death. But he'd yet to repeat the words to me. Mates for life. Shouldn't the words be given easily?

So maybe after tonight, we'd start dating—let our human side catch up with our wolf side. It seemed sort of backward, but I guessed he'd had no choice since I hadn't known the truth about my circumstances. The unknown was big and scary.

I don't know how long I walked. I walked until my legs were too tired to run away or climb the slopes that surrounded us.

Face your fears, Dr. Brandon had said.

But no way could he have known the fears that were cascading through me now. At the edge of the woods I stopped walking—and waited. The moon rose higher. I'd always found it peaceful. It had the power to change the tides, and tonight it would possibly change my life.

Eventually Lucas got up and walked over to where I waited. My knees grew weak and I was grateful that I had a sturdy tree to lean against. He lifted his arm and pressed his forearm against the bark, over my head, as though he, too, needed some sort of support. The action brought him even closer. I felt the welcoming heat of his body reaching out to mine. I'd slept nestled against that body. I knew it in both human and wolf forms. It didn't frighten me.

He dipped his head down. His lips were almost touching mine. Almost.

"Kayla," he whispered, and his warm breath caressed my cheek. "It's time."

Tears stung my eyes. I shook my head. The reality was that I didn't want to change into a wolf. It sounded painful. It wasn't how I'd ever envisioned myself. It was a gigantic step that terrified me. "I'm not ready, not yet."

I heard an ominous, throaty growl in the distance. He stiffened. I knew he heard it, too. He shoved away from me and glanced over his shoulder. That's when I saw them. The wolves had returned and were prowling the perimeter of the clearing.

Lucas looked back at me, disappointment reflected in his silver eyes. "Then pick another. But you can't go through it alone."

He turned his back on me and began striding with purpose toward the wolves.

"Wait!" I screamed after him.

But it was too late.

He started discarding his clothes with each quickening step. Then he was running. He leaped into the air—

By the time he hit the ground, he was a wolf. Always before I'd missed the transformation. He'd either shifted when I wasn't looking or he'd hidden himself. I'd expected it to be ugly. To be like it was in the movies. His body fighting the metamorphosis. Instead it had been a quick shimmer, graceful and powerful in its intensity. It had been . . . right.

He threw back his head and howled at the moon. The anguished sound reverberated through me, called to me. I wrestled against answering, but the wildness that resided deep inside me was too strong, too determined to have its way.

I started running toward him. The grass was soft and cool beneath my bare feet. He'd almost died for me. I could live without him saying he loved me. But I couldn't live without him. As I crossed the open space, I dipped down and picked up the black cloak. I continued on until I reached him. I draped the cloak over him and knelt. "I choose you."

In another shimmering blink, he was standing before me, again in human form, his body cloaked in black. I rose and smiled at him. He was a warrior, a guardian. Whether in human or wolf form, he was Lucas. He was courageous. And a year ago, he'd looked at me and known—known what I was afraid to face. That we belonged together. He'd had my name etched permanently on his skin.

He took my hand and led me to the center of the clearing. When I glanced back, the wolves had quietly disappeared. So they'd only been there to offer me options, to force me to choose. Privacy once more belonged to Lucas and me. I was relieved that they were gone. I didn't want to share this moment with an audience.

Lucas stopped walking and drew me into the circle of his embrace. And waited. Waited for me to accept him. To kiss him. In some ways, this moment was more monumental than what would follow. I lifted myself up on my bare toes. It was all the encouragement he needed. He lowered his mouth to mine.

In a way, it was like every kiss I'd ever had before. Soft and warm. In a way, it was like no kiss I'd ever had before. Hungry and wild.

In the blink of an eye—or I might have blinked if my eyes had been open, but I'd closed them with the first gentle touch—it shifted from *we're friends testing the waters* to *we're mates, our lives in each other's hands, our destinies intertwined.*

Face your fears, Dr. Brandon had told me. But how did I face this? How did I face that I felt so much for him already, that if anything happened to him, my life would be over?

Mates. Destiny. Forever.

The words were a gentle refrain going through my mind. Sure, I had choices. I could walk away, but even if I did, I thought my heart and soul would remain behind with Lucas.

He drew back from the kiss, but his arms tightened around me. He nuzzled the side of my neck and I heard him inhale my scent. I inhaled the masculine fragrance that was him.

And waited.

I waited for the moon to reach its zenith. I waited for my body to respond. I waited for unbearable pain. I waited, wondering if I'd be disappointed or relieved if nothing happened.

I felt the first caress of moonlight and my skin began to tingle. I stiffened with awareness and nervousness. Moonlight couldn't be felt and yet I felt it.

Lucas said in a low voice, "Relax. Don't fight it, but stay with me."

I felt little pinpricks, a thousand tiny jabs inside and out. I could hear my blood thrumming between my ears. I could smell the earthy fragrance of the woods and the sexy scent of the guy standing with me. I heard the rapid thudding of my heart. My toes cramped. My ankles popped.

"I love you, Kayla."

I jerked back and met Lucas's silver gaze. As far as distractions went, he was incredible.

"I couldn't say it before, not until you chose me. I love you."

He kissed me again. It was wonderful and terrifying. It was possessive and liberating.

I felt fire shoot down my spine.

"Not yet," he urged. "Stay with me. Hold on to me. Focus on my voice." He kissed the side of my neck.

I'd had cramps before, but nothing like this. It was all-encompassing, from my head to my toes. It built and built—

"Let go," he rasped. "Now, let go."

There was a burst of white, a flash of color, a concussion that made no sound, but was deafening—

Then I was looking into Lucas's silver eyes and staring at his furry face. I looked down at my paws, my legs. At the red fur washed by moonlight.

Are you okay?

It was his question, asked without words.

Yes.

He touched his nose to mine, nuzzled my neck, then my shoulder. Even though he was a wolf, I could smell Lucas, could smell the essence that was him in human form.

You're beautiful, he thought.

Only when I'm a wolf? I was a little vain.

Always. It's easier to think than to say.

I don't feel different.

It's just a shape.

I wanted to laugh. I'd been so afraid. And it had been so easy. With him beside me, it had been like stepping into silk.

Will I be sore tomorrow?

A little.

What do we do now?

We play.

What about your wound?

It's almost healed.

He pounced on me, teasingly, lightly. We rolled. We jostled.

Catch me, I thought just before I started racing across the clearing.

He gave me a head start. I loved the feel of the wind

in my fur. I loved the speed with which I traveled. I ran faster than I'd ever run.

But I couldn't outdistance him. He easily caught up with me. Then we ran together while the moonlight washed over us.

SEVENTEEN

That night I slept within the cocoon of Lucas's arms, with the white cloak around me. I'd shifted back to human form with no problem at all.

"You're a natural," Lucas had said with a hint of pride in his voice.

We'd spent a lot of time kissing and talking before we'd finally drifted to sleep.

I woke up first. The light inside the cavern was dim, but it was enough so I could watch Lucas sleep. Being here with him, sleeping beside him—I knew it was where I belonged.

Last night when I'd transformed into a wolf, all that

I'd been, all that I thought I'd ever be, had changed as well. I wasn't who I had thought I was, but strangely, I now knew myself better than I ever had before.

The fears that had resided inside me—I knew now that they were my inner beast awakening. Deep within me, I'd known a change was waiting, but I hadn't realized what it was, I hadn't known what to do.

This morning there was no fear. Not of my past and not of my future. I'd discovered my true self last night, and in the discovery my fears had dissipated.

And now I had Lucas. I was everything he'd expected, all that he wanted. And he was what I wanted.

Very quietly, I got up and walked to the waterfall.

I wondered if my mother had experienced her first shift here. Had my dad helped her through it? I tried to remember if I'd ever seen a mark on his shoulder. I was just a kid when they died. There was so much I hadn't paid attention to.

But I had reconciled my memories of the day they'd died. The transformation had unlocked my past. I could clearly see them now on that last day we were together. They'd been trying to explain what I was, what we were. I could see them looking at me and each other with love. They held no fear. For them the transformation was a celebration of what they—we—were. They'd been so focused on making certain I wasn't afraid that they

246

hadn't heard the hunters.

It had been a long time since I'd missed them. But I missed them now. I missed them terribly.

Although I didn't hear him, I knew Lucas was there before he put his arms around me and drew me back against him. Where he was concerned, my senses were more in tune since the shift.

"Are you okay?" he asked.

"I was thinking about my parents. Last summer I wasn't ready to face the place where they died." I turned within his arms and gazed into his eyes. "I think I need to do that, but I don't know where they died."

He tucked my loose hair behind my ear. "Someone in Wolford will know. Your parents were part of us."

Wolford. The place he fought to protect, where the people he guarded sought sanctuary once a year.

I nodded. I'd doubted it before, but I believed it now. Strangely, the tightening in my stomach and the nerves that always accompanied thoughts of my parents' death were absent. At long last, I was ready to deal with my past.

"Should we travel as wolves?" I asked.

"We will, but I can carry the backpack so we arrive with clothes."

"Oh, good idea." I furrowed my brow. "How do you handle that anyway—always finding clothes?"

"We have stashes hidden around. We'll set some up for you. And whenever possible, you leave your clothes where you can find them again. You'll learn it all."

It took us a day and a half to get to Wolford. It wasn't a place I could have found without a guide. It was near dusk when we arrived. I wasn't certain *village* was the right word for it.

It was a fortress, surrounded by a tall wrought-iron fence, topped with evil-looking spikes. Wolves prowled the inside perimeter. Yet for all of its unique appearance, it did manage to somehow blend in with the landscape, so I didn't really notice it until we were right upon it.

At the gate, Lucas punched numbers into a keypad and the heavy barrier slowly swung open. It appeared this place was a combination of ancient and modern.

Taking my hand, Lucas led me up the dirt path toward the large foreboding stone and brick structure. Two tiny Westies came yapping around the corner. Lucas dropped into a crouch and petted them.

"Are those really dogs?" I asked.

He laughed. "Of course."

"Can we communicate with dogs?"

"Sure. You just say, 'Sit, fetch, come.' I can teach you the commands."

Laughing, I slapped playfully at his arm. "Very funny."

"You can't read their thoughts," he said, standing back up. The little dogs raced away. "I don't even know if they have thoughts."

"I guess I have to learn to accept our limitations and think in terms of what we are, not what we aren't."

"Something like that."

I glanced around. "So, where exactly is the village?"

"There are a few buildings around, but most of it is gone except for this one."

"It looks like a huge mansion or a fancy hotel or something."

"It's large enough to accommodate people who stay when they come for the solstice," Lucas explained. "Only the elders live here on a permanent basis. The others gather for the summer solstice. That's still a couple weeks away, so there won't be many people here yet."

"No problem. I'm fine easing my way into this."

We walked up the massive steps leading to the front door. Lucas shoved it open. I was awed as we walked inside.

It was monstrously large. A grand, sweeping staircase rose from one side of the foyer. Portraits lined the walls and lights glittered through a huge crystal chandelier. It was like something out of *Homes of the Rich and Famous*.

"It's not exactly a wilderness cabin, is it?" I asked.

Lucas chuckled. "No."

"Do you live in something like this?"

"I live in a dorm."

I smiled. "You know what I mean. Did you grow up in something like this?"

"No. Grew up in a normal house."

I was still having a hard time thinking of Shifters as normal in any way.

"Lucas!" A large, booming voice sounded as a man with a mane of silver hair strode out of one of the nearby rooms—a room I could see into a little and thought was probably a parlor.

Lucas grew incredibly somber. "Dad."

This was Lucas's father? He looked like—well, quite honestly, he looked like he could be a politician. He grabbed Lucas in a huge bear hug. I could see a thin layer of tears in his eyes, eyes as silver as Lucas's.

He moved Lucas back, but kept his hands wrapped around his arms.

"I'm so sorry about Devlin," Lucas said. "I had no choice."

"It's hard, but it has been for some time now. We lost him long ago. The grief is strong, but there is also a measure of peace."

"Mother—"

"She understands. It's the way it had to be. Devlin

betrayed us and himself." He patted Lucas's shoulder with a big, strong hand. "You cannot blame yourself."

While his father's words were comforting, I knew Lucas did carry a burden of guilt for what had happened. How could he not? He wouldn't be the guy I loved if he didn't feel some remorse.

His father turned his attention to me. "This must be Kayla."

"Yes, sir."

Mr. Wilde gave me a small smile. "You remind me of your mother."

I gasped. "You knew her?"

"Indeed. Your father, too. Good people."

"Maybe you could tell me about them sometime. I have so few memories."

"We'll talk later."

"Oh, Lucas!" An attractive older woman rushed from the parlor and wrapped her arms around him. She leaned back and cupped his face between her hands. Tears welled in her eyes. "I know you're a guardian, but you're still my little boy and I was so worried about you."

"Mom, I'm sorry."

"Shh," she cooed. "You have nothing to apologize for. You took a vow to protect us at all costs. Sometimes the price is high. We know that." She hugged him again, and I could feel some of the tension easing away from Lucas.

When she released him, he stepped back, took my hand, and drew me near. "Mom, this is Kayla."

Mrs. Wilde smiled at me. "Of course it is. Welcome back to the fold, my dear."

"It's good to be back . . . I think."

"It's where you've always belonged." She hugged me. "We'll talk later. Right now, the elders are waiting for you."

Lucas and I walked alone through the huge house with our footsteps echoing around us. Finally we reached a room with life-sized statues of wolves on either side of the closed door. Lucas stopped and looked at me. "This is the counsel room," he said quietly. "Only the elders and the Dark Guardians are allowed inside."

"Then I should wait out here for you?"

"It's your choice, Kayla. You don't have to choose the life of a guardian, but I would speak in your favor if you did. I trust you with my life."

"Do I have to fight for a place?"

"You have to take an oath to serve, protect, and guard."

I released a self-conscious laugh.

"What?" he asked.

"My adoptive dad is a cop. I was thinking about majoring in criminal justice. I guess this isn't that different.

But there's so much I don't know."

"I'll teach you."

He had no doubts, and because he didn't, neither did I. "I want to do this, Lucas."

He took my hand, opened the door, and we strode into a room with a huge, round table. "Do not tell me that King Arthur—"

"Maybe. After all, he had Merlin."

I heard a squeal and turned.

"Lindsey!" I cried.

She wrapped her arms around me and hugged me tightly. "I'm so glad you're back."

Over her shoulder, I saw Brittany.

"You should have told me, Lindsey," I said. "All those emails, text messages, IMs, and you couldn't mention it?"

"You would have freaked out. You might have left and then what?"

"So you and Brittany are both Dark Guardians?"

"Apprentices. We haven't shifted yet, but next full moon . . ." She sighed. "Can't wait."

A banging on the table caught our attention. Lucas led me around to two empty seats at the table. I guessed they'd known I was coming.

It was very easy to tell who were the elders and who were the Dark Guardians. The elders were, well, elderly, and the guardians were all young and had the look of warriors about them.

An elder stood up. He had a wizened face and gray hair that touched his shoulders. "Is she one of us?"

"Yes, Grandfather, she is," Lucas said. I was slightly stunned that this man was Lucas's grandfather, but it made sense. The role of leader passed down from grandfather to grandson. "She is also my mate. Where she goes, I go."

Lucas's grandfather nodded what I thought was his approval. His pale, silver eyes focused on me. "Are you willing to take the oath?"

"I am."

He moved around in front of me. "Kneel."

It seemed an archaic ritual, but still I dropped to one knee. Lucas knelt beside me and took my hand.

"Are you sure we're not getting married here?" I whispered.

"I'm sure."

"Do you, Kayla Madison, swear to hold our secrets and to guard us from all evil and harm that may come our way?"

"I so swear."

I wasn't sure how I knew those were the words I needed to say, but the old man's eyes lit up and Lucas squeezed my hand.

"Then you are welcomed into the ranks of the Dark

Guardians," he said somberly.

I heard applause as Lucas rose and pulled me to my feet. Then, one by one, the remaining elders introduced themselves. Afterward, each Dark Guardian approached and Lucas handled the introductions. Rafe was there, of course, and Connor. There were six others whom I didn't know: four guys and two girls. When Lindsey and Brittany finished their apprenticeship, there would be twelve Dark Guardians. I supposed in time that I'd get to know the others better.

When everyone had been introduced, we took our places at the table, as did the elders.

Lucas's grandfather, Elder Wilde, then spoke to the group. "It is with great sadness that we must report that Devlin did a lot of damage with his mischief. These scientists will not give up easily. We must prepare for what is to come."

Lucas stood. "Much of the danger we now face is my fault because I hesitated to kill my brother when I had the opportunity—when I should have. I know there is some doubt about my ability to be an effective leader. If anyone wishes to challenge my right to lead, I am ready to face that challenge."

"What? No!" I came to my feet so fast that I nearly knocked over the chair. "If anyone challenges you, they'll have to get through me first."

"Kayla—"

"It wouldn't be fair. Not until your wound is completely healed. And I don't see how it's your fault that Devlin went bad."

Several throats were cleared, and I realized that I'd probably broken some protocol.

"She has a point," Elder Wilde said. "But I don't think you'll find anyone willing to challenge you."

The elder was right. No one challenged him. Which was a good thing, because I'd been serious about kicking butt if someone did. I'd just found Lucas. I wasn't going to let anyone take him away from me.

Discussion continued for a while, but the majority wanted to take a wait-and-see approach. Maybe the scientists wouldn't return. But I thought that was just wishful thinking. After a while, we were dismissed.

Later that night, after dinner, Lucas and I sat on a love seat in a grand room with a huge fireplace. His parents sat across from us.

"You can't believe how relieved we were when your adoptive parents brought you here last summer," Mrs. Wilde said. "When you and Lindsey became such good friends, we knew she'd be able to convince you to return this summer."

"Why didn't everyone just tell me everything last summer?" I asked.

"To be honest," Mr. Wilde said, "we weren't sure

what to do. You were a unique case, Kayla. We'd never had one of our own raised by outsiders. There were several other people in the woods the day your parents died. They immediately called the police, and the authorities got to you before we could. We'd never had a situation like this. We were at a loss. We did what we could to find you, but records were sealed. We have only so much influence."

I hated to think what might have happened if I hadn't come back to the woods last summer. It had been scary enough going through my first transformation with some idea of what might happen. But to have gone through it knowing nothing at all?

And my poor adoptive parents . . .

"So, my adoptive parents—I just return to them at the end of the summer and act like nothing has happened?"

"Can you do that?" Mrs. Wilde asked. "Or we could talk with them, claim to be lost relatives, arrange for you to move up here."

I shook my head. "They love me. I don't want to leave them until it's time to go to college." I squeezed Lucas's hand. "It wouldn't be fair to them. I want to let them have this last year with me that they were expecting." My adoptive mom had already made all kinds of graduation plans. I was their daughter, after all.

"They'll understand me falling in love over the summer

and wanting to go to the same college you do next year. Besides, you'll need my dad's seal of approval."

He grimaced.

"It won't be that bad," I assured him. "You both serve and protect, so you'll have that in common."

"Except I can't tell him that," Lucas said.

"But he'll sense it." My dad was good at judging people.

I turned my attention back to Lucas's parents. "Do you know the place where my parents died?"

Mr. Wilde nodded. "I'll give Lucas directions."

Before bed, Lucas and I took a walk around outside. Being in a house, even one as large as this one, had me feeling on edge. I'd always liked the outdoors, but now it meant much more to me. It was where I wanted to be.

"Are you overwhelmed?" Lucas asked quietly.

"No, your parents are nice. What if Lindsey hadn't convinced me to come?"

"I would have gone to you, Kayla."

I put my arm around him and snuggled in against him. "I thought things would change when I turned seventeen. I didn't expect them to change this much." I peered up at him. "I didn't expect to get a boyfriend."

"You've got more than that." He stopped walking and turned me to face him. He put his hand over his chest. "My heart, my soul, my life . . . they're all yours."

I felt tears sting my eyes. "I love you, Lucas."

He took me in his arms and kissed me. As always, it was wonderful and warm, and so Lucas.

As we walked back to the house, he asked, "Are you nervous about tomorrow?"

He'd gotten the directions from his father, and we were going to go to the place where my parents had died.

"A little," I admitted. "I wish you could sleep with me tonight."

Arrangements had been made for me to share a room with Lindsey and Brittany. After all we'd been through together, it seemed odd that we wouldn't be together tonight—but we were around parents and apparently Shifter parents weren't any different from Static parents when it came to how they felt about girls and guys sleeping together.

"The guardians are all here because of what happened with Mason and his group. They'll all be leaving tomorrow to head back to the park entrance. We have other groups to lead. So tomorrow, you and I won't come back here. We'll sleep beneath the stars."

"Can't wait. But we'll return for the summer solstice?"

"Yeah. In a couple of weeks."

I glanced around. "What if Mason and his group find this place?"

"We'll deal with it."

We walked back to the house. I had high hopes that tomorrow would truly unlock my past.

The next morning, Lucas and I left before dawn. We shifted so we could travel more quickly. I had to admit that I enjoyed several aspects of my wolf form. My senses were heightened, and after each transformation they remained a little more sensitive when I was in human form. I was surprised by how natural it all seemed to shift from human to wolf and back again—with little more than a thought.

I lost track of time, and yet I somehow knew when we were nearing our destination. I couldn't explain it. I slowed from a racing run to a walk—and then I halted completely. I was breathing unusually heavily and I knew it was nerves. I wasn't afraid of what I would discover.

I knew all the secrets now. But everything was going to seem more intense. My parents had died here.

Lucas noticed I was no longer keeping pace with him. Still in wolf form, he returned to my side and dropped the backpack at my feet. After he casually padded out of sight behind a thicket, I shifted and changed into shorts and a tank. I tossed the backpack his way.

It was only a few minutes before he rejoined me, in human form and dressed in jeans and T-shirt.

"It's over here," he said, taking my hand.

"I know."

He gave me a surprised look. "Do you recognize the place?"

"No, not really, and yet it's familiar."

"Dad drew me a little map of the place. He said the police reports indicated everything happened over here."

I began to get chilled as we neared a place where the brush was thick. I knew that in all these years, things would have changed. Trees would have died. Others would have grown. But there was a wall of rock with thick scrub brush along its base.

Kneeling down I parted the brush to reveal a small cavern. Images bombarded me.

Hiding.

"Be quiet, Kayla."

My parents—

Breathing heavily, I stood up quickly and glanced around.

"What is it?" Lucas asked.

"I remember. They brought me here. They wanted—" I dropped to the ground and buried my face in my hands. "They transformed. They were so beautiful. Then we heard the hunters yelling about seeing wolves . . . There were gunshots. So loud."

I fought to remember everything. Lucas knelt beside me and placed his hand on my knee.

"Don't force it," he said.

I shook my head. "No, I . . . Mommy pushed me inside that little cave. Then she changed to human form and got dressed. The hunters were drunk. They kept shooting where they'd seen wolves. It was chaos." I shook my head. I couldn't see it clearly. All I know is that my parents had been in human form when they died—because they were dressed. They'd each taken a bullet through the heart.

"I remember waiting, terrified and quiet." I looked at the small cave, now hidden. "I heard footsteps. It was one of the hunters. He found me and took me away. I guess I'll never have all the answers." I twisted around and faced Lucas. "I think they wanted to show me what we were so I wouldn't be afraid. But because of what happened, I was always afraid—because I didn't understand what they didn't want me to be afraid of."

"Are you still afraid?" he asked.

"No." I touched his cheek. "I have you."

"Always," he said.

That night we made camp near a series of small waterfalls.

Standing beneath the great black sky, I leaned my back against his chest. He brought his arms around me and dipped his head to nuzzle my neck. He was my mate. Forever.

Or at least as long as we were both breathing.

I glanced up at the moon. Already it was waning toward darkness. By the time the summer solstice arrived, it would be a tiny sliver.

There were still dangers out there. I could feel them threatening. When they arrived, I'd face them with the Dark Guardians, because now I was one of them.

But for tonight, we were safe.

I turned within Lucas's arms. He lowered his mouth to mine and kissed me passionately. The taste of him, the scent of him reaffirmed that we were alive.

For now, it was enough. For now, it was everything.

The second book in the sexy new Dark Guardian trilogy!

Dark Guardian #2:
Full Moon

Lindsey is one of the Dark Guardians, a pack of werewolves who live deep within the state park. Years ago, her parents arranged her betrothal to Connor, her childhood friend. But lately Lindsey can't stop thinking about gorgeous, brooding Rafe. In her heart, Lindsey knows that what she feels for Rafe goes beyond attraction… and her feelings won't be denied. But going against the pack could mean being cast out forever. Who will she choose?

HARPER TEEN
An Imprint of HarperCollins Publishers

www.harperteen.com

Woodland High School
800 N. Moseley Dr.
Stockbridge, GA 30281
770-389-2784